The CAPYBARA CONSPIRACY

CONSPIRACY

A NOVEL in THREE ACTS
by ERICA S. PERL

Alfred A. Knopf 🐕 **New York**

THIS IS A BORZOI BOOK PUBLISHED BY ALFRED A. KNOPF

All rights reserved. Published in the United States by Alfred A. Knopf, an imprint of Random House Children's Books, a division of Penguin Random House LLC, New York.

Knopf, Borzoi Books, and the colophon are registered trademarks of Penguin Random House LLC.

Visit us on the Web! randomhousekids.com

Educators and librarians, for a variety of teaching tools, visit us at RHTeachersLibrarians.com

Library of Congress Cataloging-in-Publication Data
Names: Perl, Erica S., author.
Title: The capybara conspiracy : a novel in three acts / Erica S. Perl.
Description: First edition. | New York : Alfred A. Knopf Books for Young Readers, 2016.
Identifiers: LCCN 2015047497 | ISBN 978-0-399-55171-0 (trade) |
ISBN 978-0-399-55172-7 (lib. bdg.) | ISBN 978-0-399-55173-4 (ebook)
Subjects: | CYAC: Theater—Fiction. | Middle schools—Fiction. | Schools—Fiction.
| Mascots—Fiction. | Capybara—Fiction. | Humorous stories. | BISAC: JUVENILE
FICTION / Performing Arts / Theater. | JUVENILE FICTION / Social Issues /
Friendship. | JUVENILE FICTION / Humorous Stories.
Classification: LCC PZ7.P3163 Cap 2016 | DDC [Fic]—dc23

The text of this book is set in 12-point Chaparral Pro.

Printed in the United States of America
October 2016
10 9 8 7 6 5 4 3 2 1

First Edition

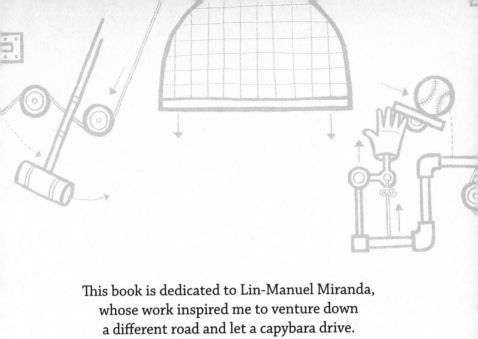

This book is dedicated to Lin-Manuel Miranda,
whose work inspired me to venture down
a different road and let a capybara drive.
Mad props, and much gratitude, ESP

**Okay, guys, you ready?
It's time. Break a leg!**

The CAPYBARA CONSPIRACY

ACT I, SCENE I—FARLEY MIDDLE SCHOOL

*Two kids are sitting in two chairs, facing the audience.
A sign behind them reads* PRINCIPAL'S OFFICE—WAIT
HERE. *There is a big bowl of apples sitting on an end
table between the chairs. One of the kids, DEV, looks a
little nervous. He is wearing a baseball cap and holding
a file folder. The other kid, OLIVE, looks more nervous
than DEV. OLIVE selects an apple from the bowl. She
polishes and repolishes it, casting sidelong glances at
DEV. Finally OLIVE can't resist striking up a conversation. She leans over and asks . . .*

OLIVE: So, whatcha in for?

DEV: Excuse me?

OLIVE: You're waiting to see the principal. What did you
do? I mean what is it that you are alleged to have done?

DEV: Me? Nothing!

OLIVE: Good! Very convincing. And I like your approach. Deny everything.

DEV: No, really! I just moved here, but my old school hasn't sent over all the forms, so now I'm stuck here until they straighten things out. My name's Dev, by the way.

OLIVE: I'm Olive. Olive Henry. I guess the fact that I'm waiting outside the principal's office might make you think *I'm* the kind of kid who gets in trouble. Well, I'm not! I only know what to do if you're accused of something because my dad is a criminal defense lawyer. Ned "Not Guilty" Henry? I'm sure you've seen his ads on TV. (*Sings*) "1-800-N-O-T-G-L-T-Y, wasn't me!" No?

DEV: (*Shakes his head*) Like I said, we just moved here.

OLIVE: Yeah, they're pretty memorable. If you'd seen one, you'd remember it. I actually wrote that jingle.

DEV: Oh yeah?

OLIVE: Yeah. I usually write plays, but sometimes, for the right terms, I'm willing to be a hired gun.

DEV: A hired what?

OLIVE: Oh! Not like that! I meant I sometimes do work for hire. Writing work! Not gun work. I've never touched a gun, and I would never hurt anyone or anything. That's why I can't believe people said I . . .

DEV: Said you what?

OLIVE: (*Carefully looking around to ensure no one is listening*) Listen, can you keep a secret?

DEV nods. OLIVE looks him over and seems to decide she can trust him.

OLIVE: They said I killed Cappy.

DEV: Whoa. Who's Cappy?

OLIVE: Seriously? You haven't heard of Cappy? The capybara?

DEV: The what?

OLIVE: Capybara. It's the world's largest rodent. Cappy is, I mean *was*, our school mascot . . . before this whole mess.

DEV: The school mascot is dead?

OLIVE: He is?!

DEV: You just said he was!

OLIVE: No I didn't. I said people said I killed him. But I didn't!

DEV: Wait a second. Isn't a mascot, like, a guy in a costume?

OLIVE: At most schools, yes. But Edmund Farley Middle School is not like most schools. At least not in the mascot department. Allow me to explain. . . .

COACH K. walks onstage, carrying or leading CAPPY on a leash to center stage, where COACH K. stops and bows. While OLIVE continues, COACH K. demonstrates with props, including a football, a sweater for CAPPY, and oversized photos.

OLIVE (CONT'D): The reason for this is that Coach Knickerbocker, better known as Coach K., who coaches Farley's football, basketball, and baseball teams, had a girlfriend . . .

COACH K. displays a photo of her.

OLIVE (CONT'D): who owned a lot of exotic pets. She skipped town, and he ended up the proud owner of the three pets she left behind:

4

COACH K. *displays a long photo of Gatie and an even longer photo of Pythie.*

OLIVE (CONT'D): a six-foot-long alligator named Gatie, a twelve-foot-long python named Pythie, and a capybara named . . .

DEV: Barry?

OLIVE: (*Shoots him a withering look*) Cappy. Pythie and Gatie went to the National Zoo.

COACH K. *puts his photos away.*

OLIVE (CONT'D): But as it turned out, the zoo had phased out its capybara exhibit—along with several other animals, like giraffes and hippos—to make more room for its elephant habitat. Or at least that's what the coach said—everybody thinks it was really that he couldn't bear to part with him. At any rate, one day Coach K. happened to swing by football practice with Cappy in the back of his truck. The team was in the midst of a six-game losing streak, and nobody could turn it around. Cappy climbed out while the coach was fixing a drippy Gatorade drum, and the next thing anyone knew, Cappy was pushing a football down the field with his nose. The whole team burst out laughing, then cheering, then raced Cappy to the end zone. It was like Cappy was the secret ingredient the team hadn't realized they were missing. And the rest is history. Cappy attended the next game on a leash, wearing a ketchup-red and mustard-yellow Farley sweater, and the team won seventeen to zip. In fact, Cappy was so popular that the team name was officially changed from the Farley Fiddler Crabs. Which, let's be honest, was a questionable mascot to begin with, right down to the costume they always made some poor sixth grader wear.

A short kid dressed up in a ridiculous crab costume enters, walking sideways, crablike.

SIXTH GRADER: Go, Crabs, go! Scuttle, scuttle, scuttle!

He exits, with COACH K. and CAPPY following him out.

OLIVE: So now the official team name is the Farley Capybaras, or Caps, represented by none other than Cappy. The fact that Farley is the only middle school in America with a capybara as a mascot—not to mention an *actual* capybara—is a huge deal. Did you happen to notice the framed *Sports Illustrated* cover in the front-foyer display case? They did a two-page spread on Cappy. It doesn't seem to matter that he looks like a shaggy oversized eggplant with legs. When Cappy's on the field, Farley teams go on to greatness. Any questions?

DEV: Yes. Why would you want to kill a giant rat?

OLIVE: Not rat, capybara. And please stop saying that! (*Sings*) "1-800-N-O-T-G-L-T-Y, wasn't me!" Look, here's what happened. It all began last Monday. Here at Farley Middle School, every day starts the same way: with morning announcements.

The bell rings and lights come up on a second area: a classroom. Students sit in two rows of chairs, all facing stage right so the students are seen in profile. The two middle chairs in the front row (closest to the audience) are empty for the time being. The chairs bracketing the two empty ones are occupied by PEP SQUAD GIRLS #1 and #2. All the kids are chatting and joking around before class starts.

When the morning announcements begin, they settle down.

PRINCIPAL HIGGLEY: (*Speaking from a microphone stand off to one side, broadcasting to the school over the loudspeaker*) Happy Monday, Capybaras! Principal Higgley here, and it's a slightly overcast day at Edmund Farley Middle School, the winningest school in Northeast Central Maryland. I have it on good authority that the fog will burn off by midafternoon. Which is great news for our undefeated boys' baseball team, facing off against Gorgonzola Prep at three-fifteen. Faculty, please note that all members of the team, as well as our fabulous pep squad, the Farley Flamethrowers, are excused from seventh period early today to give them time to suit up. The Lady Caps softball team is off today, but if you see any Lady Caps in the hall, give 'em a big hoof five on their twelve–two victory over Our Lady of Dubious Distinction!

OLIVE: (*To DEV*) I know this may sound weird, but in sixth grade I actually loved middle school. It used to make me proud to hear that we were the best in so many things: baseball, basketball, soccer, lacrosse, gymnastics, pep squad, you name it.

Each time she mentions a team, students in the class hold up balls or equipment or do something to reference their sport.

OLIVE (CONT'D):   I mean, I'm not the best at any of those things. Arguably, I'm the worst at some of them. But in sixth grade, our school's undefeated record made me feel vicariously victorious. Fast-forward to now: seventh grade. Every morning, every announcement, I've gotten a daily workout rolling my eyes, listening to the same things again and again and again.

PRINCIPAL HIGGLEY: Blah blah blah baseball. Blah blah blah pep squad. Blah blah blah hoof five.

OLIVE rolls her eyes each time to demonstrate.

OLIVE: It started to dawn on me: Farley Middle School is so sports obsessed, even the morning announcements are as exhausting as a PE class.

PEP SQUAD GIRLS #1 and #2 run over from the classroom to where OLIVE and DEV sit. They surround OLIVE, shaking their pom-poms while she eye-rolls, and escort her to the classroom, where she takes the stage-right-er of the two empty seats in the downstage row. DEV stays behind but remains the focus of OLIVE's running monologue.

PEP SQUAD GIRL #1: C'mon, let's give those eye muscles a workout. And roll those eyes! Roll 'em! Rollll . . . and again . . .

REYNALDO appears at the classroom door, late for class.

PEP SQUAD GIRL #2: You too, Delgado!

REYNALDO: *(Eyes rolling, synchronized with OLIVE)* I'm rolling, I'm rolling.

OLIVE: Hey, Rey! *(Calling out to DEV)* That's Reynaldo Delgado, my best friend.

REYNALDO: Ahem, your 100 percent gorgeous best friend.

OLIVE: (*Sarcastically, to REY*) Right, because I have six other best friends.

REYNALDO: You *wish* there were six more just like me.

OLIVE: (*To DEV*) I do wish. Then I wouldn't have to share him with the whole school. Everybody loves Rey.

REY's eye rolling has now turned into a full-body dance, in which he's accompanied by the PEP SQUAD GIRLS.

PEP SQUAD GIRLS #1 and #2: Go, Rey! Yeah, Rey! Go, Rey! Yeah, Rey!

REY dances to his seat, directly behind OLIVE, cheered on by his adoring mob of fans. PEP SQUAD GIRL #1 and PEP SQUAD GIRL #2 return to their seats.

OLIVE: (*To DEV*) Rey and I met in homeroom last year. By some minor miracle, he landed in my homeroom this year, too. Okay, it was no accident. His mom is the school administrator—

REYNALDO: And media specialist!

OLIVE: —here at Farley Middle School.

PRINCIPAL HIGGLEY: . . . which is the seventh time the Capybaras have held the state record, for those keeping score . . . heh heh, keeping score. . . .

OLIVE gets up in frustration and walks closer to DEV to complain to him.

OLIVE: (*To DEV*) See what I mean about this school not prioritizing anything but sports? Have you heard our principal say a word about the Scrabble club? The Math Maniacs? Or my beloved drama club, the Farley Follies? You haven't, have you?

DEV: Well, you know, I haven't really been . . .

OLIVE: Exactly! And what have you heard instead? Football. Baseball. Synchronized snorkeling, even, probably! Edmund Farley Middle School has a team—or several—for every sport imaginable. I know this might sound crazy, but not everyone here plays sports. (*In the direction of PRINCIPAL HIGGLEY*) What about the rest of us?

PRINCIPAL HIGGLEY: (*Ignoring her because, remember, he's on the loudspeaker and can't hear her*) . . . nineteen to nothing!

The class erupts into cheers. REY reaches out his "hoof" to fist-bump OLIVE.

REYNALDO: Don't leave me hoofing!

OLIVE starts to return to her seat, but before she can get there, PEP SQUAD GIRL #2 leans over to intercept the hoof bump.

PEP SQUAD GIRL #2:   *(To OLIVE)* Players only.

REY and PEP SQUAD GIRL #2 bump "hooves," or rather, hands curved downward to resemble a hoof. REY offers OLIVE his other "hoof" for a bump on the down low.

OLIVE: *(To DEV)* Rey is so not a player. For Rey and me, a healthy eye rolling—or a really energetic round of charades—is about as close to a workout as we're likely to get. We can't help it. I prefer theater, and Rey likes . . .

REYNALDO: Roller-skating, long showers, crunchy Cheetos, not the puffy ones . . .

OLIVE: Yeah, okay, he's got it. Since Rey is so . . .

REYNALDO: Gorgeous.

OLIVE: Stop it! I was going to say TALL. Since Rey is so tall, people presume he's got game, until they're in PE with him. He's not exactly afraid of the ball.

A crumpled-up note is passed by one of the girls to REY, who fumbles dramatically, falling out of his seat in an unsuccessful attempt to catch it.

OLIVE (CONT'D):   More like allergic to it. (*Aside, to DEV*) He's good at pretending to like sports, though. That's on account of his natural acting abilities, which is also why I cast him in all my plays. But the truth is, I'd find parts for him even if he couldn't act, because most kids at this school would rather be on deck—(*to REY*) right, that's a baseball term?

REYNALDO: You're asking me?

OLIVE: (*To DEV*)—than on the stage. Hey, do you have any interest in acting?

DEV: Uh, no.

OLIVE: You should definitely try out! Even if you have no experience and are painful to watch, I'll find a part for you. You know why? Because I am not about to be anyone's dream crusher. I've been the crushee myself on too many occasions. It makes for some very dark days.

REYNALDO: (*Rising to his knees in prayer*) Amen to that.

OLIVE: (*Helping REY back to his seat, then turning to DEV*) BUT, last Monday was not going to be one of them.

That's because I had it (*impersonating PRINCIPAL HIGG-LEY*) "on good authority" from Mrs. Delgado—

REYNALDO: My mom.

OLIVE: —that, for once, ONE of Monday's morning announcements would be 100 percent sports-free. I knew because I wrote the script and slipped it to Mrs. Delgado with three fun-sized 100 Grand bars taped to the envelope.

REYNALDO: Smart. My mom will do almost anything for Olive. But tampering with the morning announcements definitely calls for sweetening the deal.

OLIVE: Want to hear what I wrote? Take it away, Rey.

REY jumps to his feet and impersonates PRINCIPAL HIGGLEY, using a pencil as the mic.

REYNALDO: (*Clearing his throat*) Ahem! This just in . . . another victory, this time by our *creative* Capybaras. Olive Henry, a seventh grader, has received a blue-ribbon citation in the statewide playwriting competition for *Nevermore/Hush,* an imaginative mash-up of Edgar Allan Poe's "The Raven" and Margaret Wise Brown's *Goodnight Moon.* This qualifies her to enter a new play in the Super Bowl of scripting: the National Festival of the

Performed Word, which will be held later this month in Orlando, Florida. Let's all put our hooves together in a round of applause for Olive Henry!

OLIVE bursts into enthusiastic applause. DEV claps as well, to be polite. REY accepts the applause, then returns to his seat.

OLIVE: That was awesome, Rey! (*To DEV*) Did you like how my script hit all the important notes? One, a non-athlete can still hit it out of the park; two, a girl—me—who will never be excused from seventh period early to suit up for anything can still do something impressive and noteworthy; and three, that girl is going to *Florida*!!! (*She stands up to do a little victory dance and sing that last word.*)

DEV: You won a trip to Florida?

OLIVE: (*Modestly*) Yeah. Now, I knew that 90 percent of the kids who tuned out at the word "creative" would perk up at the sound of the word "Orlando." But still, just having it announced was going to be a major victory for us non-jocks. I was so ready for everybody to be like, "Wow, maybe I should write plays like Olive!" "Hey, do you have any tryouts coming up, Olive?" "Can we interview you for the *Farley Fanfare*? We're holding the front page for you, Olive!"

OLIVE is still standing, and she has wandered off in her reverie. PEP SQUAD GIRL #1 tugs on REY's sleeve.

PEP SQUAD GIRL #1: *(Loud enough so OLIVE can hear)* Who's Olive?

OLIVE: *(To DEV, with a sigh)* Yeah, well, they would have said all those things last Monday if the morning announcements had gone the way they were supposed to. Here's what happened instead.

OLIVE takes her seat in the classroom again as the morning announcements continue.

PRINCIPAL HIGGLEY: Sorry to be going long this morning—um, at any rate, I know we have a busy day, so let me just wrap things up here. Let's see, what else? Oh! Right.

OLIVE: *(To REY)* This is it!

PRINCIPAL HIGGLEY: This just in . . . I am pleased to announce another victory, this time by a new Capybara club making a distinctive break from recreational to competitive play. Our Ultimate Frisbee club, the Sky-Caps, took down the squad from Marion Barry Middle School with speed and precision yesterday, establishing their dominance on the field. For this reason, the Extra-curricular Oversight Committee unanimously voted that the SkyCaps will no longer be meeting in the Academic Dimension. Instead, they will practice in . . . the auditorium! They will also be provided with the opportunity to sell concessions at Caps baseball games! Oh, and it seems we also have some sort of a writing contest winner here, named . . . Henry . . .

OLIVE: (*Rising to her feet and speaking in the direction of PRINCIPAL HIGGLEY*) What? No! Not Henry. Olive! Olive Henry.

PEP SQUAD GIRL #1: That's what he said.

OLIVE: No he didn't. He said . . .

PRINCIPAL HIGGLEY: Henry Oliver! Let's put our hooves together in a round of applause for ALL our winners! Thanks for listening up; now let's get out there and kick today's butt.

OLIVE: Unbelievable!

BOYS #1 and #2: (*Guffawing and elbowing each other*) Heh heh! He said *butt*!

REYNALDO: (*To BOYS*) News flash: he always says butt. It's practically his tagline. Remember last month? When we had those state tests?

PRINCIPAL HIGGLEY: Let's get out there and kick those Maryland-mandated exams' butts!

REYNALDO: Or during School Nutrition Week?

PRINCIPAL HIGGLEY: Let's get out there and kick the federal nutrition pyramid's butt!

REYNALDO: Or when we had that anti-bullying pep rally?

PRINCIPAL HIGGLEY: Students, I challenge you to get out there and kick bullying's butt!

OLIVE sits down again, glumly.

OLIVE: Oh geez, that's probably why he doesn't like me. Remember my editorial in the *Farley Fanfare*? I criticized him for that anti-bullying pep rally.

REYNALDO: You weren't the only one who thought having the baseball team take their bats to a piñata labeled "bullying" was in questionable taste.

OLIVE: Yeah, but I was the only one who wrote about it. Under my own byline, remember? "Olive's Oasis"?

REYNALDO: No offense, O? But that particular watering hole was located on the back page, waaaay below the fold.

OLIVE: You're saying nobody read it?

REYNALDO: No! My mom put it on the fridge.

PRINCIPAL HIGGLEY: Please rise to salute the flags.

Students stand while FLAGS march in and position themselves around OLIVE, who stands like her classmates, hand over heart.

FLAG #1:   I am the flag of the United States of America. Stars and Stripes forever.

FLAG #2:   I am the flag of the great state of Maryland. I am the only state flag in the United States to be based on English heraldry.

FLAG #3:   I am the flag of Edmund Farley Middle School. I feature the school colors, ketchup red and mustard yellow, and a cartoon likeness of Farley's team mascot, Cappy the Capybara. Go, Caps!

Students softly mumble their way through the Pledge of Allegiance while OLIVE and REY recite their own oath, which can be heard above the rest.

OLIVE: I pledge allegiance to the arts . . .

REYNALDO: and my ability to survive this sports-obsessed middle school . . .

OLIVE: so I can go on to greatness . . .

REYNALDO: somewhere else . . .

OLIVE: with liberty and justice for all kids . . .

OLIVE and REYNALDO: not just jocks.

PRINCIPAL HIGGLEY: One more thing, students. Don't forget, this Friday we'll have a very important pep rally in honor of the birthday of a very special someone . . . Cappy, our beloved school mascot! We're doing this because here at Farley we recognize that in school, as in life, some things are more important. And by more important, you know what I'm talking about . . .

ALL STUDENTS EXCEPT OLIVE and REYNALDO: (*In unison, on cue*) Sports!!!

Students hoof-bump, then sit down. The FLAGS march off. REY reaches over, holding out a hoof for OLIVE to bump.

REYNALDO: Don't leave me hoofing, Henry!

OLIVE: It's not funny.

REYNALDO: It's kind of funny. Principal Higgley calling you a dude and all.

OLIVE: That's not the point!

REYNALDO: I know, but it's either laugh or cry. If there were a competition for the most sports-obsessed school in the state of Maryland, this school would win, hooves down!

BOY #1: (*Perks up at the sound of the word "win"*) Did you say "win"? You know it! Wooo! Undefeated!

OLIVE: And to top it off, they gave *the auditorium*—you've heard of it: big room *with a stage, best rehearsal space in school*?—to the Ultimate Frisbee club!

REYNALDO: Yeah, that's messed up! Aw, but you know how it's going to go. Give it a few weeks. As soon as those Frisbee kids fall off the stage and end up on crutches, Principal Higgley will come to his senses.

OLIVE: Rey, who are we kidding? I could go to Florida and win the grand prize at the National Festival of the Performed Word. And you know what that would mean to Principal Higgley and all the jocks at this school? Exactly nothing.

REYNALDO: Even if they gave you a big trophy? Principal Higgley's a sucker for a big trophy.

OLIVE: You know what, Rey? I'm tired of playing nice. I'm tired of selling tickets that nobody buys to plays that nobody sees performed on stages that aren't actually really stages! And PS, playing nice isn't really getting us anywhere. Is it?

REYNALDO: Well . . .

OLIVE: EXACTLY! Look, Rey. It's time to do something radical. Something that will get this school's attention, big-time.

REYNALDO: Oh no. You're getting that crazy look, Olive. Count me out.

OLIVE: I knew I could count on you, Rey! I knew you wouldn't want to miss out on the chance to make history.

REYNALDO: By being the first son of a school administrator—and media specialist—to be expelled? No thanks.

OLIVE: Don't just think about yourself, Rey. Think about all the kids here who are suffering from, um, coordination-ism. Every kid who can't catch or throw or look cute in a uniform is being persecuted. And meanwhile, they're getting ignored for the things they excel at . . . things like . . .

As she names each interest, a kid who pursues it gives a little wave or gesture of affirmation (for example, when she says "artists," two kids reveal that they are secretly painting or drawing in their notebooks).

OLIVE (CONT'D):   Art and music and . . .

REYNALDO: Scrabble and coding . . .

OLIVE: Right! And yoga and writing . . .

REYNALDO: Yeah, and math and interpretive dance . . .

PEP SQUAD GIRL #2 gets up and does an interpretive math dance, e.g., with a calculator or abacus or adding machine trailing paper.

REYNALDO (CONT'D):   Wow, I always thought those were two separate clubs. Good to know.

OLIVE: And so many other cool things. Don't you want this whole school to sit up and say, "Hey, wow. What you nonathletes are into is actually as awesome as anything happening on a field—if not possibly more awesome."

REYNALDO: Yeah, of course I want that. But how?

OLIVE: I've actually given this a lot of thought.

REYNALDO: That's what I was afraid of.

OLIVE: The answer is obviously theater. Political theater.

REYNALDO: Olive, no one at this school is into regular theater. What makes you think they'd buy tickets for a play about politics?

OLIVE: I'm not talking about putting on a play. I'm talking about staging a coup. You know, like the Glorious Revolution, in 1688? Or Napoleon's coup within a coup, in 1799? Or Che Guevara, the Cuban Revolution, 1956? Are you ever awake in history class?

REYNALDO: It's not my fault. I get sleepy after lunch.

OLIVE: It's like Che Guevara said:

Spotlight on CHE, who enters holding up an apple.

CHE: The revolution is not an apple that falls when it is ripe. You have to make it fall.

CHE tosses the apple to OLIVE.

OLIVE: Thanks, Che! You see, Rey? "Liberty and justice for all kids, not just jocks!" We need to make the apple fall.

OLIVE holds out the apple to REY, who accepts it reluctantly.

REYNALDO: But what if the apple gets all bruised and mushy when it falls?

OLIVE: We'll be fine, Rey. We're not the apple. We're the ones shaking the apple tree. I'll explain everything at our Follies meeting after school.

REYNALDO: I dunno, O. I've got a bad feeling about this. I don't see it ending well.

OLIVE: Relax! What could go wrong?

REYNALDO: Um, everything?

Undeterred, OLIVE takes the apple from REY, polishes it on her shirt, and takes a big bite. BLACKOUT.

ACT I, SCENE II—FARLEY MIDDLE SCHOOL

Back at the principal's office waiting-area chairs, REY is now sitting next to DEV, where OLIVE once sat.

REYNALDO: How long has she been in there?

DEV: A long time.

REYNALDO: That's not good. Did Olive tell you how this whole mess started? Last Monday's morning announcements and the showdown in the Dungeon?

DEV: The Dungeon?

REYNALDO: (*Jumps up and starts pacing*) She's got to stop blaming herself! The truth is, there's one person to blame for everything that went wrong. And that person is not Olive. What kills me is that when we met Pablo, we thought he was the answer to our prayers. Not our worst nightmare.

It all started after school that very same day, Monday. We were in the Dungeon, getting ready for a drama club meeting.

Across the stage, in the area where the classroom was set up, we see the school basement. The chairs are now grouped in small clusters of two to four. A prominently placed sign reads WELCOME TO THE ACADEMIC DIMENSION, WHERE CREATIVITY GETS A WORKOUT! *The words* "ACADEMIC DIMENSION" *have been crossed out with red paint, and over them it now reads* DUNGEON. *OLIVE is setting up a circle of folding chairs next to a whiteboard that reads* FARLEY FOLLIES MEETING 3:15 P.M. *REY and DEV walk over to join her.*

OLIVE: On the bright side, with the Frisbee kids gone, the Dungeon is a much better place to work.

26

REYNALDO: (*To DEV*) As you can see, the Dungeon is not, in fact, an actual dungeon. It is a large, windowless storage space in the school basement, where all of the nonathletic clubs have to have their after-school meetings. The school calls it the Academic Dimension to make it sound cool and exciting, as if that will keep us from noticing that we're all stuck in a dark, dingy basement.

PRINCIPAL HIGGLEY enters, carrying a cup of punch. He raises it, addressing the audience.

PRINCIPAL HIGGLEY: As principal of Farley Middle School, I hereby dedicate this space and name it the Academic Dimension. Any and all clubs looking to explore nonathletic pursuits outside of school hours are invited to meet in the Academic Dimension between the hours of three-fifteen and five p.m., Monday through Friday. Yes, that's right, all of you at once in the same cramped space. I now invite you to join me for refreshments, including these delicious hoof-shaped cookies left over from last week's JV soccer tournament. That will be all. Oh, and let's kick some *academic* butt!

PRINCIPAL HIGGLEY exits.

REYNALDO: The location isn't the worst part about the Dungeon, though. It's . . .

Well, you'll see.

Students march in, carrying signs indicating their affiliation: FARLEY FANFARE, ROBOT REBELS, MATH MANIACS, MAD SCIENTISTS, CODING CADETS, ORFF ENSEMBLE, GREEN SCENE, YES FOR YOGA, *etc. They all begin to work on their projects simultaneously, yelling to be heard over one another and getting in one another's way.*

REYNALDO: (*Shouting over the din*) And, until today, the Ultimate Frisbee club practiced here, too. Picture that, if you will.

Two Ultimate Frisbee players enter and start tossing discs across the room, yelling "Sorry!" "Heads up!" and "Watch out!" as the discs fly at and above students trying to do yoga, math, and Orff ensemble.

REYNALDO (CONT'D):   This made it hard for the Farley Follies, our school drama club, to rehearse. Even though there were usually only two of us at rehearsals—until that afternoon, when suddenly everything changed.

REY walks over to OLIVE and helps her continue to set up before they both sit down together. Meanwhile, PABLO is walking around the Dungeon, looking at things. PABLO is handsome, with a backpack hanging casually from one shoulder. OLIVE notices PABLO, elbows REY, and they start whispering. DEV continues to watch from the periphery.

OLIVE: You see that kid? Does he look familiar to you?

REYNALDO: Yes. He's in our homeroom.

OLIVE: Huh. That must be it. I wonder what he's doing down here.

REYNALDO: He's probably one of my many admirers. Bet you a Fresca!

OLIVE: I wouldn't be surprised. He's definitely not a Dungeon dweller. He's cute. And not just Dungeon-cute. Cute-cute.

REYNALDO: You can say that again. Oooh, look out, he's coming this way!

REY dives under a chair.

PABLO: Excuse me. Is this where the Farley Follies meet?

OLIVE: Rey, get up. (*To PABLO*) Do you mean the Farley *Foilers*?

REYNALDO: (*To DEV*) It's a common mistake. The fencing club meets in the gym now. Ever since an unfortunate incident with the Yes for Yoga club.

BOY #2, wearing fencing gear and holding a sword,

enters from one side, thrusting and parrying his way through the room.

YOGA KID: Namaste—yeouch!!!

BOY #2: Sorry! Ooops! You okay? Coming through!

BOY #2 exits, foil held high.

PABLO: No, not the Foilers, the . . . *Follies.* It's a club for people who do plays?

OLIVE: You're in the right place. I mean, that's us. I'm Olive and this is Reynaldo.

PABLO: Hey! I'm Pablo. I'm in your homeroom. I couldn't help but overhear you talking this morning.

REYNALDO: *(Happily punching OLIVE)* I knew it! You owe me a Fresca.

OLIVE: *(Punches REY back before addressing PABLO)* You heard us talking about what?

PABLO: Everything. You talk a lot. You write plays, yes? And you won an award, no?

OLIVE: Yes. No. I mean yes, yes! *(To REY)* He knows I write plays!

REYNALDO: 'Cause that's what drives middle school boys wild with desire. Playwriting!

PABLO: And you said you need a place to practice your plays. But instead of giving the auditorium to you, they gave it to some sports guys.

ORFF ENSEMBLE KID: Okay, let's try that again on the count of three. One and a two and a . . .

They begin striking their instruments with felt mallets.

YOGA KID: Ommmmmm . . . Ommmmmmmm . . .

MATH MANIAC KID: The square root of pi is the logical starting place for this next puzzler. . . .

OLIVE: Shall we adjourn to our conveniently located (*air quotes*) "black box theater"?

Covering their ears, PABLO and REY both nod and follow her into an area marked SUPPLY CLOSET. *(This can be indicated by an archway.) Inside, they huddle near cardboard boxes marked* GLUE STICKS *and* MARYLAND-MANDATED MIDDLE SCHOOL EXAM ANSWERS—DO NOT OPEN UNTIL MAY.

OLIVE (CONT'D): Ah, much better! Now, you were saying?

PABLO: I heard what you said this morning, and I am here to help you.

OLIVE: Help us what?

PABLO: With the political theater. And making the apples fall. I want to help you execute your plan.

OLIVE: You do?! I mean of course you do. Everyone wants in on our plan.

REYNALDO: They do? Since when? And what plan?

OLIVE: But how do you think you can help us?

PABLO: Simple. By kidnapping Cappy.

OLIVE: Wait . . . what?

PABLO pauses dramatically. Outside the door, the Orff ensemble delivers a drumroll.

PABLO: Kidnapping Cappy. You know Cappy, yes? The Farley Middle School mascot, who is actually a real live animal?

OLIVE: Yes, we're aware of who Cappy is. Big, furry, lovable old Cappy.

REYNALDO: Big, furry, terrifying old Cappy.

OLIVE and REY look at each other, surprised.

OLIVE: Cappy? Terrifying?

REYNALDO: Cappy? Lovable?

PABLO: Yes, Cappy. By taking him, you'll turn the tables on them. It's a brilliant idea. I wish I had thought of it.

REYNALDO: Kidnap Cappy? Are you out of your mind?

OLIVE: Yeah, we can't do that!

REYNALDO: Nor do we want to do that.

PABLO: That's not what you meant when you said you were going to shake the tree and make apples fall?

OLIVE: No! Not at all!

PABLO: Oops. My bad. Never mind. *(Hands in the air, he begins to back away.)*

OLIVE: Why would you think we wanted to do something like that?

PABLO: Forget I mentioned anything. It's a bad idea. A crazy idea. And definitely too ambitious for you.

REYNALDO: Beyond crazy.

OLIVE: I like things that are ambitious.

PABLO: And even though the rewards would be HUGE, there's definitely a tiny little bit of risk involved.

REYNALDO: Exactly—way too much risk.

OLIVE: Huge rewards?

REYNALDO: Olive, WAY too much risk.

OLIVE: Right! Of course. But, just out of curiosity, how much risk? And do you mean risk to him? Or to us?

PABLO: No one would actually be at risk. You'd take Cappy, and he'd be completely fine the whole time. Then all you'd need to do would be return him safely and say you found him. Returning the missing mascot would make you heroes. They'd do anything to thank you.

REYNALDO: Like let me get PE credit for my roller skating?

OLIVE: Or even better, like let the Farley Follies rehearse in the auditorium.

PABLO: Please. They'll name the auditorium after you. With a plaque and everything.

OLIVE: Ooh, a plaque.

REYNALDO: Hold on a second. That still doesn't sound completely risk-free to me. Plus, how are we going to look like heroes if we're the ones who took him in the first place?

PABLO: No one has to know that. And no one will suspect you because no one kidnaps their own team mascot. Rival teams take mascots. Haven't you ever seen *Ace Ventura*?

REYNALDO: Pablo, can Olive and I have a word alone?

PABLO: Of course.

PABLO steps out of the supply closet.

REYNALDO: *Ace Ventura?*

OLIVE: You got me. We don't have cable.

REYNALDO: No, that's not the point. You're not seriously considering doing this?

OLIVE: I don't know. Maybe?

Meanwhile, PABLO's cell phone rings. He answers it. (OLIVE and REY continue to talk, but we don't hear them because the focus is on PABLO . . . who OLIVE and REY can't hear because they're still in the closet.)

PABLO: Mami? How you doing? Yes, I'll be home late. You know, because of baseball practice, like always. (*Pause*) You want to bring cookies for my coach? (*Panicking*) Nah, that's not a good idea. Why? Oh, uh, I mean, I'm already the coach's favorite. We wouldn't want the other guys to get jealous, you know? Okay, sure, see you later. Love you, Mami!

OLIVE: Pablo said it'll all be okay. We'll return him safely and get to be heroes.

REYNALDO: If it's so easy, why does he need us? Why doesn't he just do it himself?

OLIVE: Why do you have to be so suspicious, Rey? Maybe he wants to be friends? Maybe we inspired him to do something he's wanted to do for a long time and he doesn't want to leave us out?

REYNALDO: Olive, he's been in our homeroom since September. He hasn't said two words to us all year, and now all of a sudden he wants to be our BFF? It's hardly like I'm unapproachable.

OLIVE: You have a point.

REYNALDO: So how are we going to figure out what his angle is?

OLIVE: Well, for starters, we could ask.

OLIVE and REY stick their heads out of the door to address PABLO.

OLIVE (CONT'D):   Hey, Pablo? Don't take this the wrong way, but why do you want to help us? I mean, what's in it for you?

PABLO: You've never been to a Farley Caps baseball game, have you?

OLIVE: I have not.

REYNALDO: Me neither.

PABLO: Then you've never seen me play baseball, have you?

OLIVE: Nope.

PABLO: That's what I thought. It's because I don't play baseball! I don't play sports at all. I am a total loser, just like you guys! And as a loser, I am tired of watching all the winners win. It's time for us losers to come together and form our own team. By taking Cappy, we can show them that losers can be winners, too.

REYNALDO: Hey! (*Pulling his head back inside the door angrily*) Reynaldo Delgado is no loser.

OLIVE: (*Unconvinced*) O-kay.

PABLO: (*Seizing his chance*) Can I make a confession? That's not the only reason.

OLIVE: It's not?

PABLO: Uh-uh. I like your style, Olive. I feel like, with your creativity, we'd make a great team and change the world.

OLIVE: (*To PABLO, reading into what he is saying*) Yeah, we would. Thanks! (*Pulling her head back in, she speaks to REY*) See? It makes more sense now, doesn't it? He's like us guys!

REYNALDO: You mean us losers?

OLIVE: Rey! Pablo meant that's how the school treats us, not how he sees it.

REYNALDO: Even so, do you seriously think Pablo's plan is a good idea?

OLIVE: You got a better plan?

REYNALDO: Any plan that doesn't involve kidnapping a capybara is, by definition, "a better plan."

OLIVE: What's so bad about giving his plan a try?

REYNALDO: I just don't know if we should trust him. I mean, think about it: He says he's "like us," but we've never seen him in the Dungeon before today. And, also, doesn't he look like he plays sports?

OLIVE: Rey, I don't know every kid who comes to the Dungeon, and neither do you. And are you seriously suggesting we should make assumptions about him based on how he looks?

REYNALDO: Okay, fine, you're right. But there's still the problem of what happens if we get caught. My mom will kill me.

OLIVE: Look, my dad may be the best criminal defense lawyer in town, but I don't want to get in trouble any more than you do, Rey. Still, what's the alternative— doing nothing? Don't you want to win a major victory, not just for us but for—

REYNALDO: I know, I know . . . "all kids, not just jocks." I've still got a bad feeling about this. Plus, you know

I don't like that Cappy. He's supposed to be a giant hamster or something, but he looks like a chupacabra to me.

OLIVE: Chupa-wha-wha?

REYNALDO: Chu-pa-ca-bra. It's a creature of the night, a goat sucker. Don't you read the weekly *News of the Weird*? (*Shakes his head*) And you call yourself well-read. They come in darkness and they slit your throat and drink your blood like one of those bats or something. They were sighted in Baltimore, like, last year. You can look it up!

OLIVE: So, let me get this straight. You don't want to do this because you're afraid Cappy is a vampire?

REYNALDO: Possibly. Plus, if my mom ever found out . . . When she gets mad, there's nobody scarier.

OLIVE: Rey, you're my best friend. So if you don't want to do this, I'm not going to make you.

REYNALDO: Wow, Olive, that's amazing. The truth is, I really don't want to. . . .

OLIVE: Pleeeeeeease!!! I'll never ask you for anything again, never ever ever.

REYNALDO: Ugh! Fine. As long as I don't have to touch that . . . thing. I'm telling you, it's a chupacabra.

They come out of the storage closet and reconvene with PABLO.

OLIVE: We have two stipulations. That's lawyer talk for stuff you need to say yes to. One: if anything goes wrong, we protect each other. If we all deny everything, none of us can get in trouble.

REYNALDO: And two: nothing can go wrong, because my mother will kill me.

PABLO: Okay. That all works for me.

REYNALDO: Wait, one more. Three: I don't have to touch it. I mean him. I mean Cappy.

PABLO: Got it. No problem.

PABLO puts out his hand to shake. OLIVE looks at REY. REY nods, somewhat reluctantly. OLIVE extends her hand, then REY does, so they pile their hands one on top of the other, sports-team style.

OLIVE: (*Joking around*) Hoof five, everyone!

REYNALDO: Yeah, we should make up a cheer or something.

OLIVE: How's this? One, two, three! Cappy conspiracy!

Lifting and lowering their pile of hands, they repeat OLIVE's chant together twice, finishing by raising all their hands in triumph.

PABLO: Excellent. This is perfect. There's a baseball game at seven. We'll kidnap Cappy tonight!

They run offstage together, talking excitedly.

ACT I, SCENE III—FARLEY MIDDLE SCHOOL

OLIVE has returned to the principal's office waiting area. She and DEV are sitting next to each other again.

OLIVE: So . . . what did Rey tell you while I was in there?

DEV: Some stuff about a kid named Pablo?

OLIVE: Yeah, Pablo made things a lot worse. It's one thing to say you're going to, uh, borrow your school's mascot. It's another thing to actually do it. For starters, as we discovered while researching capybaras on the Internet, the world's largest rodent is, by definition, large.

She shows an image on her phone to DEV, who recoils in horror.

DEV: What the heck is that?

OLIVE: It's a capybara sitting in a swimming pool filled with fruit. Isn't that cute?

DEV: (*Unconvinced*) Looks like a hippo crossed with a bunny. A really hairy hippo-bunny. Why is it taking a fruit bath?

OLIVE: I have no idea. What can I say? That's the Internet for you. Which is why Rey and I decided it was also important to do some primary-source research.

Across the stage, REY appears with binoculars, watching CAPPY from a stealth hiding position.

OLIVE (CONT'D): That's how we discovered that when the particular capybara in question is a school mascot, he spends most of his time with the coach and/or on the field. And we learned that capybaras that have not been raised in a loving home since infancy can be, well, temperamental.

REY pulls back from his binoculars, looking shocked at what he has seen, and pointing.

REYNALDO: Cappy bit Coach K.! I told you I had a bad feeling about this!

As OLIVE keeps talking to DEV, we see COACH K., wearing a bandage on his wound, leading CAPPY back to his office while scolding him.

OLIVE: *(To DEV)* Obviously we didn't know any of this stuff when we signed on. We certainly didn't know that, come Monday night, we'd be hiding in the bushes outside Farley Middle School, waiting for Pablo to give the signal that the coast was clear and we could sneak into Coach K.'s office to grab the you-know-what.

OLIVE goes to join REY. OLIVE and REY position themselves strategically, hiding in the bushes. DEV watches from the principal's office waiting-area chairs, though OLIVE periodically goes over to him or calls out to him.

OLIVE (CONT'D):   *(To REY, in a loud whisper)* Do you even know what the signal is?

REYNALDO: No. Remember? Pablo said he could do bird-calls, so we left it at that.

PABLO: *SQUAWK! TWEET-TOO-WEET! SQUAWWWWK!*

REYNALDO: Do you think that could be . . . ?

OLIVE: Yes, of course. Quick, before he does it again. If any actual birds are in the vicinity, they're probably dying of embarrassment.

OLIVE and REY duck out of the bushes. PABLO, dressed all in black, emerges near the side door to the school.

PABLO: Oh good, you came. I was worried you'd chicken out.

OLIVE: No way! We're fine. You can tell because I talk a lot when I'm nervous. And as you can see, I'm fine. I don't know the meaning of the word "chicken." I mean, I do, but I just . . . I laugh in the face of danger. *(She dissolves into nervous laughter.)* Ha ha ha ha ha!

REYNALDO: Olive! *(Mimes "stop it")*

OLIVE: *(While PABLO and REY talk, OLIVE confides in DEV.)* What was wrong with me? Good question. Sure, Pablo was cute, but it wasn't just that. There are other good-looking boys at Farley, but all of them are jocks, which means they're completely not interested in me. And I am not interested back! I have zero interest in boys who nod off in class while I'm doing an oral report, or who make yammering clam mouths *(she demonstrates)* with their hands to their friends when they think I'm not looking.

DEV: Well, it's possible that—

OLIVE: (*Interrupting him*) I'm not blind. I know what kids at this school think of me. When I win a Tony or an Oscar or a Pulitzer for my work, they'll beg for my autograph and brag that they knew me when. But now? As far as they're concerned, the dryer lint from their team uniforms is more fascinating than I am. (*She pauses to gaze at PABLO and swoon.*) Pablo is different. He's the first boy who ever asked me to work on a project and wasn't after just one thing: a better grade. Pablo was interested in me. And cute. It was like a math problem. Cute plus interested in me divided by not a jock equals, well, I'm not sure what it equals . . . some sort of X factor, obviously. But I've taken enough algebra to know that, in this case, I was definitely excited to solve for X.

PABLO and REY, with OLIVE joining last, enter the building and move cautiously down the darkened hallway.

PABLO: Coach K. always leaves his office door unlocked.

OLIVE: (*Confiding in DEV again*) I also liked that he knew stuff! Now I can see that he knew too much stuff. Like that Coach K. always leaves his door unlocked. Or when he said there'd be a baseball game at seven. Who knows that kind of stuff?!

DEV: Kids who play sports?

OLIVE: Yeah, sure, I know that now! But way back then, I was innocent. Naïve. A mere child, practically.

DEV: Didn't you say this happened last Monday?

OLIVE: Exactly!

They push open the door to COACH K.'s office and are greeted by a bizarre tweeting noise.

OLIVE (CONT'D):   (*To PABLO*) Okay, okay. Enough with the birdcalls.

PABLO: That's not me. That's him.

REYNALDO: Him?

They find the light switch. There, tied to a radiator, is CAPPY sitting in a wading pool full of muddy water, next to the coach's desk. His hooves are more like paws with long toes. He almost looks like a dancer on pointe. A rotund, hairy dancer with buckteeth, but a dancer nonetheless. His dark brown fur is stiff and bristly, more warthog than teddy bear. And he's wet, obviously, from sitting in the tub.

REYNALDO (CONT'D):   (*Terrified, hiding behind OLIVE*) Chupacabra!

OLIVE: (*To CAPPY*) Hey there. Aw, you're actually kind of cute. Rey, just look at him. Seriously, you're like ten times as big as he is. And only a fraction as hairy.

REYNALDO: (*Reluctantly peeking out*) Ugh . . . He looks like a giant, hairy, big-nosed troll.

Without them noticing, someone has appeared from the shadows. It's a girl, pointing something long and dangerous-looking in her sweatshirt pocket at them.

BRIE: Freeze! I'm serious. Put your hands up, and nobody move. Back away from the capybara.

REYNALDO: Wait, which do you want us to do? Not move or put our hands up?

OLIVE: Or back away from the capybara, which we can't do if we're not moving. Omigosh, is that a gun?

REYNALDO: I'm too young to die!

BRIE: I guess you should have thought of that before you came here to molest this poor innocent creature!

REYNALDO: What's she talking about? We're not here to molest anyone.

OLIVE: He's telling the truth! We're not here to hurt Cappy. We're actually here to, um . . .

BRIE: Liberate him?

REYNALDO: No!

PABLO: Yes!

OLIVE: Maybe?

BRIE: Well, why didn't you say so. *¡Viva la revolución!*

BRIE sits down, reveals that the pointy thing she's been holding them with is a carrot, and takes a big bite before breaking off a piece for CAPPY, who eats it.

OLIVE: *¿La revolución?*

BRIE: *¡La revolución!* The day when everyone finally realizes that animals deserve equal rights. I'm Brie Greenberg. I'm guessing you've heard of me? Or my organization? *(She hands OLIVE a card.)*

OLIVE: *(Reading)* "'Gabriella "Brie" Greenberg, Founder and President.'" Is it "up cuddle" or "You Pee cuddle"?

BRIE: Neither. It's P-CUDL. The first "U" is silent. It stands for the Pony and Capybara Understanding and

Dignity League. I founded it when I was eight to promote respect for ponies. Since starting middle school here at Farley, I've expanded to include capybaras.

OLIVE: What's the silent "U" for?

BRIE: (*Turns beet red*) Okay, fine! When I first started the group and convinced my parents to get me the domain name, I included unicorns. Also, the "c" that now stands for "capybaras" used to stand for "cutie-pies." Did I mention I was eight? (*Clears her throat and brightly tries to change the subject*) At any rate, I try to check on Cappy most game nights to ensure he isn't being harmed or harassed. Being an animal-rights advocate, I'm always prepared to spring into action. Sorry if I frightened you.

OLIVE: Who would want to harm or harass a capybara?

BRIE: It's not so much that people want to. . . . They just don't know any better. Education is a big part of my work. I spend a lot of time explaining that using animals as mascots is exploitation.

REYNALDO: But isn't Cappy the coach's pet?

BRIE: Pet? Far from it. Soapbox, please.

From offstage, a small box from a bar of soap is sent her way.

BRIE (CONT'D):   Bigger soapbox.

A larger box is slid over to her. She stands on it.

BRIE (CONT'D):   That'll do. Live animals should not be used as mascots at sporting events and school functions. Think about it. An arena filled with bright lights, screaming fans, flashing cameras, and loud noises is terrifying and distressing for animals. Cappy's not the only one—there are owls, dogs, eagles, wolves, and feral pigs forced into slavery by sports teams all across the country. After a few years, they develop anxious behaviors and are often euthanized because they can no longer cope with the stress of the life they've been forced into.

PABLO: *He's* stressed-out? Do you have any idea the kind of stress the ballplayers are under? Run faster, throw harder, hit more runs . . . and then you do all that and make yourself crazy trying to please your coach and your mother and everyone, and you still get cut. (*Suddenly realizes that he's said too much*) I mean, that's what I've heard.

OLIVE: Wow. I had no idea about any of this. I mean, I know sports are competitive. I just thought everyone who played sports did it for fun. I guess I even thought Cappy enjoyed it.

BRIE: He's a capybara. His idea of fun involves interacting with other capybaras in his natural habitat. Not dancing in front of a crowd.

REYNALDO: He can dance?! Oh, sorry. Exploitation. Never mind.

BRIE: No offense, but if you didn't know any of that, why are you trying to liberate Cappy?

OLIVE: (*Trying to stall for enough time to make up a good reason*) Oh, that. Well, we probably shouldn't tell you. It could be dangerous. I mean, not for him, but for you.

BRIE: Dangerous? How?

PABLO: Don't look at me. (*Points at Olive and Rey*) This was their idea.

REYNALDO: Our idea?! Now wait just a second—

OLIVE: (*Jumping in*) Hang on, hang on. I can explain! Well, this particular capybara, uh, whose real name is . . . (*Looks to REY and PABLO for help*)

REYNALDO: Boppy?

OLIVE: Boppy? (*She clearly hates this suggestion.*) Fine! *Boppy* was actually stolen from his home at the Happy

Capybara Sanctuary in Buenos Aires and smuggled into this country in exchange for illegal . . .

PABLO: *¿Queso blanco?*

OLIVE: *(She likes this suggestion better.) Queso blanco.*

BRIE: The cheese? Hey, are you making fun of my name?

OLIVE: No! Seriously, my name is Olive. I would never.

REYNALDO: Yes! I mean, yes, its street name is "the cheese," but it is actually an extremely potent narcotic drug. You understand what we are telling you? And why this is so dangerous?

BRIE: I think so. But how does that involve you guys? You're in, what, seventh grade?

OLIVE: Exactly! Who would suspect seventh graders of helping ensure the safe passage of a stolen capybara?

BRIE: Hmmm . . . *(She scrutinizes the three of them.)* I guess that makes sense. Were you recruited for this rescue effort by the Capybara Liberation Front?

OLIVE: *(Guessing)* Uh, no?

BRIE: Yeah, I didn't think so. If they were involved, they would've come to me. I'm definitely the best-known capybara crusader at this school. Not that I would jeopardize my credibility as an animal-rights activist by getting involved with anyone I didn't know I could trust. *(She looks them over suspiciously.)* I can trust you, right?

OLIVE: *(Feeling guilty)* Look, the thing is—

BRIE: Okay, fine! You've convinced me. I'll do it.

REYNALDO: Do what?

BRIE: Work with you, of course. You guys seem nice, but let's be honest—you're clearly kind of clueless in the ways of the animal-liberation world. You need someone like me to guide you. I'm like an animal-rights ninja: experienced, discreet, and willing to put my life on the line, if necessary. Plus, I know aikido! *(She demonstrates.)*

OLIVE: Wow. Um, Brie, will you excuse us for a moment?

OLIVE, REYNALDO, and PABLO huddle while BRIE continues to strike warrior poses.

OLIVE (CONT'D): What do we do now? I really think it might be a good time to come clean and get out of here.

REYNALDO: Yes! I'm all for that! Except . . . she seems a little unhinged. Who knows what she might do if she finds out we're not actually here to "rescue" Cappy?

PABLO: We're not going to find out. Because we're not going to tell her.

REYNALDO: We're not?

PABLO: We're not. It's bad enough having the two of you involved. I should have listened to my brother. He always says, "If you want something done right, you have to do it yourself."

REYNALDO: My mom has a saying kind of like that. Only it's "Do I have to do everything myself around here?!" She can be kind of dramatic. She gets that from me.

OLIVE: (*A little hurt*) I thought we were working together, like a team or something.

PABLO: (*Reassuring*) We are, we are. But three's company and four's crowded, you know? We can use her help, sure, but we can't tell her the truth.

OLIVE: Why not?

PABLO: Because she'll blow our cover. Then we'll all be in hot water.

REYNALDO: What if she figures it out anyway? Then what?

PABLO: She's not going to. Besides, if we have to, we can always take care of her later.

OLIVE: "Take care of her later"? Meaning . . . ?

They freeze as the sound of the Farley marching band playing the school's fight song reaches their ears.

PABLO: That's the theme song of the Farley Flamethrowers! They twirl their flaming batons during the seventh-inning stretch, right before they bring Cappy onto the field. They'll be coming to get him any minute now.

REYNALDO: Ooh, I always wanted to be a halftime performer.

PABLO: This is baseball. Halftime's football, dude.

REYNALDO: Halftime, quarter time, three-quarter time . . . it's all good.

PABLO: Come on. We've got to get out of here!

REYNALDO: How? I am not touching that . . . that . . . chupacabra.

BRIE, who has been eavesdropping, sees her chance to rejoin the conversation.

BRIE: It's pronounced CA-PY-BAR-A. And don't worry, I've got it. *(She reaches over and wraps both arms around him.)* We don't call it P-CUDL for nothing. Come here, you cuddly boy. *(She sits down almost immediately with CAPPY on her lap.)* Oof! My, you're heavy! *(To CAPPY)* Who's a big boy? Who's a big boy?

OLIVE: Okay, let me . . . *(She tries to lift CAPPY.)* Wow, you're not kidding. That leaves you, Pablo.

PABLO: I've got a better idea.

PABLO points at a wheelchair sitting in the corner of the coach's office, next to a collection of crutches. Pulling it out, he positions it next to BRIE and guides her, still holding CAPPY on her lap, into it. Then he grabs a Farley Caps blanket and wraps it around them. Both faces, BRIE'S atop CAPPY'S, peer out.

OLIVE: This is not going to work. You look like a kangaroo. If there's one thing I know, it's that costumes can make or break a performance.

REYNALDO: Shhh! Did you guys hear that?

They freeze, listening, as we hear the distinctly peppy voices of the PEP SQUAD GIRLS, who appear at the other side of the stage.

PEP SQUAD GIRL #1:   Omigosh, that was fierce!

PEP SQUAD GIRL #2:   So fierce!

PEP SQUAD GIRL #1:   We were on fire.

PEP SQUAD GIRL #2:   Totally on fire. I mean, not literally on fire, but still.

PEP SQUAD GIRL #1:   Right! Not literally on fire. Figuratively on fire.

PEP SQUAD GIRL #2:   Exactly! See, I told you English class would come in handy at some point. SO hot!

PEP SQUAD GIRL #1:   English class is SO hot.

PEP SQUAD GIRL #2:   Brendee, not English class. Us! The Flamethrowers are so hot! Our moves are so hot. And the crowd is totally going to lose it when we do our flaming hot pyramid with Cappy at the top.

PEP SQUAD GIRL #1:   Totally! I just hope Cappy doesn't lose it when we put him up there.

PEP SQUAD GIRL #2:   He won't. He was really chill when we did it at practice.

PEP SQUAD GIRL #1:   Uh, Krystee? We used a stuffed animal in practice. The reason we're going to the coach's office is to get the real Cappy.

PEP SQUAD GIRL #2:   Omigosh, no wonder he was so quiet. (*Calling offstage*) Coach K.? Should we go and get the real Cappy, like, now?

COACH K. (OFFSTAGE):   Sure, girls. He's in my office. The door is unlocked, so just get Cappy and bring him straight to the field.

OLIVE: It's coming from over here. (*Picking up walkie-talkie from the coach's desk*) Oh geez, we're picking up audio from the coach's headset. The Flamethrowers will be here any minute!

The PEP SQUAD GIRLS exit peppily.

BRIE: (*Wrapping her arms protectively around CAPPY*) Let's do this.

PABLO: Go, go, go!

REY grabs the handgrips on the wheelchair and, pushing, leads the others out. They reenter from the other side of the stage. OLIVE doubles over, trying to catch her breath, near the principal's office, where DEV still sits.

DEV: Then what happened?

OLIVE: (*When she finally is able to speak*) I don't know. It all happened kind of fast.

BRIE: Wait, what? Don't you have a plan? Isn't there an established safe house?

OLIVE: Safe house? (*Glances nervously at REY*) Look, Brie, I've got to come clean. The reason we're here tonight is I wrote a play. Maybe you saw it? It was called *Nevermore/Hush*? It received strong reviews.

REYNALDO: Which you also wrote.

OLIVE: NOT true. You wrote them—and they were awesome.

REYNALDO: Aw, go on! No, really, go on.

OLIVE: They were great. Very little editing needed—I merely punched them up a little. (*To BRIE*) At any rate, the Farley Follies—that's our drama club—helped develop my play through our workshop series this past fall, and then it was selected to receive a blue-ribbon citation, which I'm sure I don't have to tell you—

BRIE: Cut to the chase. What does this have to do with Winston?

OLIVE: Winston?

BRIE: Yes. Cappy and Boppy were his captive names. I am giving him a more dignified name.

PABLO: Well, you've got a lot of options. Couldn't get much less dignified than "Boppy."

OLIVE: (*Aside, to REY*) Ironic, isn't it? We're here fighting for her right to do what she loves—her whole animal-rights-activism thing. Yet if we tell her the real reason we're taking Cappy, she'll bust us, and our revolution will never happen.

REYNALDO: Yeah, but, Olive, we need to tell her something. That cheese story isn't cutting it. Whew! (*Waves his hand in front of his nose*)

OLIVE: A "cutting the cheese" joke, Rey? Really?

REYNALDO: (*Still waving his hand in front of his nose, then sniffing himself*) No. Our story stinks, and now so do we. We smell like chupacabra.

PABLO: (*To OLIVE*) You like to make up stories. So make up a story.

OLIVE: Fine. (*To herself*) Okay, I can do this. Make up a story.

PABLO: A good story. A convincing story.

BRIE: (*To CAPPY, nose to nose*) From now on, you shall be known as Winston Churchill Huckleberry the Third.

OLIVE: (*Nervous and clearly making it up as she goes along*) The point is, Brie, until today, I've been too busy with my silly play to make arrangements with the safe house. So, this morning, when I called the animal underground railroad, the receptionist said, "Oh my goodness, how I wish you had called yesterday! I just gave up the last bed available to a mongoose that was rescued from a notorious mongoose-hoarding situation in Northern Virginia. If you can just hang on another few days, I'm sure something will open up, and until then we'll keep you at the top of our waiting list."

PABLO: (*Impressed*) Not bad.

REYNALDO: (*Unimpressed; to PABLO*) Seriously? (*Whispering to OLIVE*) How is that not just manure piled on top of manure?

OLIVE: (*Whispering back*) What? I think she liked the details.

REYNALDO: Maybe we should just cut our losses and take him back right now?

OLIVE: How? We can't just drop him off on the school doorstep with a note—"Please look after this capybara?"

BRIE: Over my dead body! We're all that stands between Cappy—I mean Winston—and a life of mascot misery. Let's take him to my house. We can keep him in my stables until he can be relocated to the safe house.

BRIE points the way and leads the charge, with OLIVE in the rear. OLIVE pauses before exiting.

OLIVE: (*To DEV*) That's right. She said her stables.

ACT I, SCENE IV—BRIE'S STABLES

OLIVE, REY, and PABLO stand at the doorway to BRIE's garage (use an archway if you'd like) and gape at the scene inside, with DEV still staying at the principal's office. The garage floor is entirely covered with a mixture of hay and wood shavings, and it is subdivided into about eight to ten areas by small wooden gates, so it does sort of resemble a horse paddock, except in miniature. In each of the pens are one to three small furry animals resembling CAPPY, except again, in miniature.

OLIVE: Okay, not what I was picturing when you said stables.

REYNALDO: It's actually exactly what I was picturing . . . only smaller.

BRIE: Pretty great, right? My parents asked me what I wanted for my bat mitzvah, and I said eighteen guinea pigs. We're Jewish, and eighteen in Hebrew is *chai*, which is also the word for "life," so it's sort of a lucky number in Judaism. I figured they'd go for it. They didn't. But in the end, they let me get thirteen instead, since it's also kind of a lucky number in Judaism. Part of the deal was that they'd build me these stables to keep my herd out of the house. So, everyone, meet my herd. This is Flora, Dora, Lorna, Esmeralda, Imogene, Rita, Gloria, Maisy, and Daisy. Over there are the boys, Arnold, Irving, Clark, and Mr. Pickles. Herd, this is everyone.

PABLO: Did you know they eat those in South America? Roasted on sticks.

BRIE: Please! Don't get me started on that—I'm a vegan, obviously. And don't talk about it in front of them.

PABLO: Why? Do they speak English?

BRIE: Of course not. But I read books to them, so they actually understand more than most people realize.

OLIVE: Aren't your parents going to notice that you have *fourteen* now and that one member of your herd is a LOT bigger than the others?

BRIE: Oh, they never come out here. As long as I don't bring them into the house, they're fine. Plus, my parents travel a lot. In fact, I think that's why they ended up saying yes to the guinea pigs—so I'd have someone to talk to. And probably so I wouldn't notice that my parents are never around. No wonder I like animals more than people, right? Can you bring Winston around the side?

PABLO complies, herding him from behind over to the side door. OLIVE follows him, standing nearer to where the principal's office waiting-area chairs are so she can periodically talk to DEV. Meanwhile, BRIE goes off to get the accommodations ready for her new guest.

PABLO: (*To OLIVE, as soon as they are out of BRIE's view*) There is something seriously wrong with that girl!

OLIVE: (*To DEV*) Okay, it's true that Brie seemed a little off. But I have to admit that I was feeling kind of conflicted. I mean, Brie might have been . . . eccentric, but she clearly cared about Cappy. I mean, Winston Churchill Whatever-She-Was-Calling-Him-Now. The more disconcerting part was not knowing what Pablo meant about taking care of her later.

BRIE: (*Appearing at the side door*) See, there's one big stall back here. It's big enough for a pony, even—wishful thinking!—so it should work for Winston just fine. (*To CAPPY*) Right, buddy? Look how happy you are! Free from your captors. How does that feel? We'll get you a pool to poop in, and you'll be all set.

REYNALDO: And to think all these years I thought pools were specifically for not pooping in. . . .

BRIE: Yup, capybaras don't like to do their business on dry land. Little-known fact.

REYNALDO: Little-known fact that some of us wish were even littler known.

PABLO: Okay, I'm going to call it a night. See you later, Cappy.

BRIE: Winston.

PABLO: (*Awkwardly*) Winston.

OLIVE: We should probably get going, too.

REYNALDO: Yes! (*Exaggerated yawn*) It's late.

BRIE: Okay, see you tomorrow. (*Calling after them*) Don't worry about Winston. I'll take good care of him. I might even sleep out here to make sure he settles in with the herd.

OLIVE, REYNALDO, and PABLO start walking home.

REYNALDO: I'll say it again: I don't have a good feeling about this.

OLIVE: What? You're afraid that Cappy might have his eye on those guinea pigs for a little midnight snack?

REYNALDO: Or worse! He might have a taste for a little Brie and crackers to go with them. Anything's possible.

PABLO and REY freeze and do not finish walking off-stage. OLIVE turns to address DEV.

OLIVE: (*To DEV*) At the time, I thought Rey was worrying for nothing. To my mind, things couldn't have worked out better. The next day, everyone at school would be freaking out. By Wednesday, or Thursday at the latest, we'd bring Cappy back and get a heroes' welcome. I could close my eyes and picture it already. . . .

She leaves the others to go to the principal's office, where COACH K., PRINCIPAL HIGGLEY, and MRS. DELGADO join her. OLIVE does not sit in the chairs; rather she stands and interacts with the adults while DEV watches from the chairs.

COACH K.: I can't thank you enough for bringing Cappy home.

MRS. DELGADO: Olive, look this way and smile! *(She snaps a photo.)* Oh, I'm so proud of you kids.

PRINCIPAL HIGGLEY: Because of your heroic efforts, you kids have earned the Symbolic Keys to Farley Middle School. Symbolic because they're much bigger than actual keys and they don't open any locks, but they DO represent that we'll grant you anything you wish for.

OLIVE: Oh, you don't have to do that. We were only doing what anyone would have done.

PRINCIPAL HIGGLEY: Nonsense, young lady. You kicked this missing-mascot mystery's butt! Our school needs to find some way to express our appreciation to you and your friends.

OLIVE: Well, it's not like we need a plaque or anything—unless you insist. We'd just love to get some rehearsal time in the auditorium. You know, the big room with the stage, where the Frisbee club practices?

PRINCIPAL HIGGLEY: Is that all? It's yours! Frisbee kids, back to the Dungeon.

FRISBEE KIDS walk across the stage, heads down, carrying Frisbees. FRISBEE KID #2 is on crutches.

FRISBEE KID #1: Dude. Harsh.

FRISBEE KID #2: Nah, it's all good. Fewer chairs to trip over down there.

COACH K., PRINCIPAL HIGGLEY, and MRS. DEL-GADO follow them out.

OLIVE: (*Calling after them*) Actually, you might want to let them play outside. You know, on an actual field. Just a thought.

OLIVE rejoins REY and PABLO, who unfreeze.

REYNALDO: There's just one little problem. What makes you think Brie's going to give him up without a fight?

PABLO: She'll be fine. It's like it said on a T-shirt my brother used to have: "If you love something, set it free."

OLIVE: Aw, that's kind of sweet.

OLIVE smiles at REY as if to say "See!" She exits first.

PABLO: (*To REY*) And then, on the back, it said: "If it doesn't come back, hunt it down and kill it."

REY looks concerned. REY and PABLO follow OLIVE offstage.

ACT II, SCENE I—FARLEY MIDDLE SCHOOL

REY and DEV are back on the chairs by the principal's office.

REYNALDO: When I got home that night, I was so jumpy. I knew I wouldn't be able to sleep! There was only one thing that would help me calm down anytime soon . . . some quality time in my happy place. Come with me, if you will.

REY walks across the stage and enters his bathroom (which can be an archway). DEV gets up to follow him, but REY stops him at the door.

REYNALDO (CONT'D):   Dude. Do you mind?

DEV: Oh! I thought I was supposed to . . .

REYNALDO: I'm not going to stop talking to you, but, you know . . . it's the bathroom.

DEV: No problem.

DEV returns to the chairs but keeps focused on REY.

REYNALDO: Much better. Okay, where was I?

DEV: It was late, you were jumpy, you went to the bath-room . . .

REYNALDO: My happy place, right! I looked in the mir-ror and all I could think was, "Ugh! I just don't know about that guy." (*To himself in the mirror*) Not you, gor-geous. You know who I'm talking about. *Pablo.* (*Sniffs indignantly*) If that really is his name.

Reynaldo's sister MAYA enters and approaches the bathroom door.

MAYA: (*Banging on the door*) Rey? Hurry it up in there. People are waiting!

REYNALDO: In a minute, Maya! (*Brushing his teeth*) Pablo! Paaaa-blo. (*Impersonates him*) "Hey, I'm Pablo." (*Spits out toothpaste*) Pfft! (*To DEV*) My own mother would trade me for him. And who could blame her? Handsome, smooth, and yet, there's something strange about him. I told Olive I didn't trust him. But does anyone listen to me?

MAYA: I listen to you! Every day, singing in the shower! What choice do I have? Get out of the bathroom!

REYNALDO: (*To MAYA, through the door*) I just got in here, sis! Hold your horses! (*To DEV*) They should have listened to me about the chupacabra. I know a thing or two about chupacabras. When I was little, I took a book out from the library once about a monster like that. I got scared, so I didn't ever finish it. (*He shudders.*) I couldn't even sleep with the book in my room, and after it went back, my sisters kept talking about the monster, the monster. And even though I knew they were messing with me, it still seemed really real. Then, fast-forward to last year when I heard it on the radio: they found one in Baltimore, a real monster. Only they called it something different. They called it . . .

REY tunes the bathroom radio until he gets the news report he's looking for. NEWSCASTER enters and uses the microphone stand or podium that PRINCIPAL HIGGLEY used earlier.

NEWSCASTER: A fox with mange.

REYNALDO: Yeah, okay, but hang on. Later on in the broadcast they also said it was . . .

NEWSCASTER: . . . suspected of perhaps being possibly related to a mythical creature known in Hispanic folklore as the "chupacabra," or goat sucker.

REYNALDO: See! What'd I tell you? Plus, if anyone was going to keep a chupacabra for a pet, it was that lunatic Coach K. Dude had it out for me. Called me—

COACH K. enters, passes MAYA, and bangs on the bathroom door.

COACH K.: Yo, Rey!

DEV: Doesn't everyone call you Rey?

REYNALDO: (*To DEV*) Yes, I know. Wait for it.

COACH K.: Rey of sunshine, I'm talking to you. (*Blows whistle*)

REYNALDO: Hilarious.

DEV: It is kind of funny.

REY glares at him.

DEV (CONT'D): (*Correcting himself*) Okay, it's not funny.

MAYA: (*To COACH K.*) Hey, do you mind? There's a line here. Wait your turn.

COACH K. gives one more blast on his whistle, then puts his hands up and exits—he's no match for MAYA.

MAYA (CONT'D):   Come on! You run us out of hot water again, I swear I'm gonna—

REYNALDO: In a minute, Maya! Now, where was I?

REY continues with his bathroom rituals—tooth-brushing, styling his hair, etc.—in no apparent rush while MAYA grows increasingly frustrated outside the door.

Lights come up on OLIVE, who has taken a seat in the principal's office waiting-area chairs, next to DEV. DEV turns and gives her his attention. As she talks, OLIVE gets up and walks around, clearly speaking to herself as much as to DEV.

OLIVE: After I got home that night, I tried to fall asleep, but I just couldn't. Too many thoughts were going through my head. I thought about texting Pablo, but I didn't have his number because we weren't, like, friends yet. I mean, maybe we were, but the week before he didn't even know I existed. Crazy how your whole life can change in twenty-four hours, huh? Less, even!

It could've just been that he was so handsome and exciting. . . . I'd never hung out with someone like that. I could tell that Pablo's soul was the soul of a true artist. And the fact that he knew about my plays and wanted to help me get attention for them . . . No wonder I couldn't sleep! I wondered what he was doing . . . and whether he was thinking about me . . . dreaming about me. . . .

OLIVE yawns and wanders offstage. Lights come up on the principal's office waiting-area chairs, where PABLO has snuck in and is now sitting next to DEV, in the seat OLIVE vacated. DEV jumps in surprise when he hears PABLO's voice.

PABLO: Hey.

DEV: How long have you been sitting there?

PABLO: Too long.

DEV: *(With a sigh)* Yeah, me too.

PABLO: Let me guess. You've heard their side of this?

DEV: I didn't really ask to, but yeah.

PABLO: That's cool. You should just know there's more than one side to every story. *(He gets a faraway look.)*

As PABLO talks, his brother, LUIS, enters from the other side of the stage, tossing a baseball in the air and catching it in his glove.

PABLO (CONT'D): *(To DEV)* The day I got kicked off the

baseball team was the worst day of my life. (*Pauses, grins*) Yeah, you heard me right. I play baseball. I'm a sports guy. A jock. My brother, Luis, he was like a baseball god to me, and let me tell you, I prayed at that altar. Luis was the best. He got signed to play in the minor leagues at sixteen—

LUIS: Fifteen! Two weeks shy of sweet sixteen. Crazy!

PABLO: (*To DEV*) We were still living in the Dominican Republic at the time, and you know what he told me when he got the news? He said—

LUIS: If everything goes according to the plan, you will, too.

LUIS practices pitching, getting ready for a big game. MRS. FUENTES (Pablo's mother) comes out to iron clothing while watching him proudly.

PABLO: (*To DEV*) Only everything didn't go according to the plan. After Luis got tapped to move up, I watched him play exhibition games in the Dominican Summer League. Mami was so proud. She started packing up the house and telling everyone who would listen that the family would be off for America any day now. She was thinking Florida, because that's where spring training happens, and I was sure she had already planned out where we'd go when Luis hit the Rookie League, then Class A, then Double-A, and Triple-A, and then finally

77

the majors. She ironed all his baseball gear, even his socks. She was ready, and you know what? So was I.

Luis was not. He had problems with his arm. Then he had problems with his mouth. He was telling off the ump, telling off the coach, telling off everybody—except Mami, 'cause nobody tells off Mami. And so before Florida, before the whole thing even began, it was over.

MRS. FUENTES walks away from her ironing board in stunned silence. She sits in a chair. LUIS goes to her. They pantomime along with PABLO's descriptions.

PABLO (CONT'D):   Mami was so sad. She sat in the ballpark, waiting for the manager to come out.

MRS. FUENTES: (*To LUIS, stubbornly*) I don't care how long I have to wait. I have a thing or two I need to say to this manager of yours.

LUIS: He's not my manager anymore. So what good's it going to do now? It's over. It's time to go home.

PABLO: (*To DEV*) Mami wasn't going to take this lying down. She had made a plan to go to America, and she was going—baseball or no baseball. She used her whole savings and then some and bought the plane tickets.

Mami's people were in Maryland, so we came here. She got a job cleaning offices.

When we got to the States, we were so poor, I didn't know how we were going to make it. You couldn't live in America like you could in the DR. For one thing, it got cold in Maryland. For another thing, if you were like Luis, trouble hopped on a plane and followed you. Which is why Luis ended up getting locked up.

LUIS goes behind bars. MRS. FUENTES dissolves into tears.

PABLO (CONT'D): Mami was heartbroken, but what could she do? It wasn't like the DR. It wasn't even like baseball—just two strikes and Luis was out. So I decided then and there that it was up to me. I could help by playing baseball more and more, and better than ever, playing for the both of us. When I started at Farley, they had a great team, so it seemed like the perfect thing.

Until I got cut.

Maybe it was on account of my grades, but I don't think so. I think he could smell Luis's curse on me. I knew it the minute Coach K. called me into his office.

PABLO leaves DEV to go to COACH K.'s office, where

COACH K. is at his desk, with CAPPY sitting beside him in his wading pool.

PABLO (CONT'D):   You wanted to see me, Coach?

COACH K.:   Hmm? Oh yes, have a seat.

CAPPY: *Wheeeek!!!*

COACH K.:   (*To CAPPY*) Enough already! All day and all night, *wheek, wheek, wheek!* You're making me crazy, you hear me? Put a sock in it, for crying out loud. (*To PABLO*) Not you, kid.

PABLO: Sure, Coach. Listen, I know my game's been a little off lately. If you need me to stay after practice, work harder, just say the word. You name it, I can do it.

COACH K.:   That won't be necessary, kid. I called you in because this is the end of the line for you, for now. Pains me to say it, actually. I'd love to keep you on the team, and if you had the grades, it would be a different story.

PABLO: Please, Coach K. Don't cut me. I'll work twice as hard. Ten times as hard. You don't understand. I need to stay on the team!

COACH K.:   It's not the end of the world. Take a break, hit the books, bring up your grades, and we'll talk next season, okay? Look, if I had all the money in the world? No problem. I could keep a roster a mile long and kids could keep coming to practice while pulling their grades up. But I don't have unlimited resources, kid. And there are a lot of ballplayers at this school who might not be as talented on the field as you but who consistently hit it out of the park academically. Means I have to make some tough decisions sometimes. Wish it didn't have to be this way. Sorry, kid.

COACH K. walks off, scratching PABLO's name off his clipboard. LUIS, who has been lingering in his cell, calls out to his brother.

LUIS: Just like it was with me, bro.

PABLO: Don't say that! I'm not like you. And I'm not going to break Mami's heart like you did.

LUIS: Oh yeah? How are you not going to do that? You heard the coach. You're off the team.

PABLO: (*Frustrated*) I'll figure something out.

MRS. FUENTES: (*Calling out from her ironing board*) Pablito? You're going to be late for practice. Here, I ironed your uniform.

PABLO: *Gracias,* Mami. *(He takes it and accepts her affectionate ruffling of his hair before she exits.)*

PABLO returns to DEV.

PABLO (CONT'D): *(To DEV)* I decided there was only one thing to do: get myself back on that team before she ever found out I was off it. How? Simple. By letting her think I was still on the team. By coming up with a foolproof plan to make me into a hero overnight. And by finding just the right fools to go along with it . . . and to take the fall if things went wrong!

BLACKOUT.

ACT II, SCENE II—FARLEY MIDDLE SCHOOL

REY is now sitting in the principal's office waiting-area chairs with DEV.

REYNALDO: *(To DEV)* So, the next morning . . . well, let's just say a whole poolful of capybara poop hit the fan.

OLIVE enters, on the way to her locker, followed by BRIE.

BRIE: Olive! Hey, Olive, wait up.

OLIVE: Brie! Did you see the sign out front? Everyone's talking about the mysterious disappearance of Cappy!

BRIE: Yes, well, after a very stressful evening of being liberated, Winston settled in decently, ate well, and even seemed to enjoy socializing with my herd. Thanks for asking!

OLIVE: Who? Oh right, *Winston*. That's great. (*Exaggerated*) Whew, what a relief!

BRIE: Anyway, what sign?

OLIVE: You know, the one out front that usually says "Go, Caps, Go!" or lists upcoming game times? Check it out now:

Sign walks on. It reads REWARD! FOR INFO!! TO HELP RETURN CAPPY! BELUVED FAMUS CAPYBARA MASCUT!!! *It pauses and poses before walking off.*

BRIE: I take it they're out of certain letters?

OLIVE: Yeah. Though they're never at a loss for exclamation marks. Hey, should we be seen talking to each other? You know, on account of the situation?

BRIE: Oh! Yeah, probably not.

They turn their backs on each other, continuing to talk over their shoulders.

BRIE (CONT'D):   So, I've left several messages for the CLF.

OLIVE: The CLF?

BRIE: (*Stage whisper*) The You-Know-What Liberation Front. No reply yet, but I'll check again after school and keep you posted.

REY enters, looking alarmed.

REYNALDO: Olive! I've been looking all over for you!

BRIE: (*Turning in his direction to say hi*) Hi, Rey. (*Suddenly realizing and turning back*) Oh wait, I don't know you.

REYNALDO: (*Confused*) O-kay. Olive, my mom says Principal Higgley needs to see us in his office.

OLIVE: What? Why?

REYNALDO: I don't know!

BRIE: (*Loudly*) Ooh, look at the time. I should really get to class. (*Whispers before she exits*) I'll talk to you guys later.

OLIVE: (*To REY*) Don't panic. It could be nothing.

REYNALDO: Yeah, or it could be something.

OLIVE: Should we go together? Or would it look more suspicious if we went together?

REYNALDO: How am I supposed to know?!

OLIVE: What about Pablo and Brie? How come they aren't getting called in?

REYNALDO: I don't know! Would you like me to ask my mom? "Hey, are Pablo and Brie getting called in? Because, you know, they were in on this, too."

OLIVE: Okay, okay. Look, we both know what to do. Stipulation number one! Deny everything. You say you were with me, and I'll say I was with you. And my parents were out last night, so we say we were at my house. That's our alibi. But whatever you do, Rey, don't panic. Interrogators can smell fear.

REYNALDO: Who, me? What makes you think I'm going to panic? You know what runs in my veins?

OLIVE: Hair gel?

REYNALDO: Ice water! You watch and see. I'm smooth like a fresh jar of Skippy.

He takes an interrogation seat under a bare bulb. A group of trench-coated thug types in hats and dark sunglasses congregate, collars up, backs to the audience. When they turn, it is revealed that they are PRINCIPAL HIGGLEY, COACH K., and MRS. DELGADO.

REYNALDO (CONT'D): (*Babbling nervously to interrogators*) I don't know what you're talking about! I was with Olive! I was at Olive's house! I would never go near a chupacabra. I'm afraid of them! Mom, tell them about the library book with the monster at the end.

PRINCIPAL HIGGLEY: That's not what the girl said.

REYNALDO: What? What did she say?

COACH K.: Things are not looking so good for you.

REYNALDO: What's that supposed to mean?

COACH K.: I don't know, Rey of hope. You tell me.

MRS. DELGADO: (*Shaking her head*) I knew that girl was trouble.

PRINCIPAL HIGGLEY: We've had our eye on her for some time.

REYNALDO: Olive? Why? She's, like, an honor roll student and she writes plays for fun.

PRINCIPAL HIGGLEY: Who's Olive? Oh, you mean Henry? Yes, we talked to her, too. Interesting kid. Very . . . dramatic.

Across the stage, OLIVE sits in an identical chair under an identical bulb. She is clearly in a separate interrogation area.

OLIVE: (*Sings dramatically, based on the song from the musical* Annie) "It's a hard-knock life for me. It's a hard-knock life for meeeeee. . . ."

PRINCIPAL HIGGLEY: Yeah, that girl is an odd duck, all right. But the one I'm talking about is that Greenberg girl. Gabriella Greenberg.

REYNALDO: Gabriella? Brie?

Lights go out over OLIVE as lights come up on BRIE. BRIE sits in another identical chair under another identical bulb.

BRIE: Animals are not property. Animals should not be made to suffer the indignities of mascot-dom. I made a promise to Winston that he will not be returning to his life of oppression. And I intend to keep it, no matter what!

PRINCIPAL HIGGLEY: (*Shaking his head in disbelief*) There are a surprising number of weird kids at this school.

Lights go down on BRIE, and focus returns to REY's interrogation.

MRS. DELGADO: Look, Rey, you're in a whole heap of trouble. Best thing to do is confess now. Otherwise, you're facing hard time in detention filing paperwork in the main office after school.

REYNALDO: But, Mom, I didn't do anything. I told you, I was with Olive! (*Turning to the coach and principal in desperation*) Haven't you guys seen *Ace Ventura*? Isn't it the rival team who always kidnaps mascots?

COACH K.: Well, naturally, that was our first thought. But that was before we discovered the ransom note. (*He holds up the note and reads.*) "'I took Cappy and I'm not giving him back. Sincerely, Reynaldo Delgado.'"

REYNALDO: I didn't write that! Do you honestly think I would be dumb enough to write a ransom note and sign my name?

COACH K.: We thought of that, too. Then we saw this: (*He reads.*) "'P.S. Don't blame Olive. She had nothing to do with this.'"

REYNALDO: (*Grabbing the note from COACH K. in frustration*) Okay, for the last time, I didn't write this! But you know what? Maybe Olive did! Who else would write a note blaming me and letting her off the hook?

PABLO walks on the stage, just barely. He knocks on the door to where REY is being interrogated.

PABLO: Excuse me. Principal Higgley? Can I see you for a minute?

PRINCIPAL HIGGLEY, COACH K., and MRS. DEL-GADO exit REY's interrogation and join PABLO, who walks on more, revealing that he is holding a leash, and at the end of his leash is CAPPY. OLIVE and REY leave their interrogation rooms and exit in the other direction, without seeing what has happened.

COACH K.: (*Dropping to his knees*) Cappy! It's you! There's my little buddy!

PABLO: I got up early this morning and I went to the park near my house to work out, like I do every day, and when I got there I found him, just standing there. . . .

PRINCIPAL HIGGLEY: Incredible! You say you just found him?

PABLO: Exactly. He was looking cold and hungry. So I threw him a granola bar (*he demonstrates, posing in a pitching position*), and while he was eating it, I put a leash on him and brought him here. I knew you'd be worried about him, Coach K. Did he run away or something?

PRINCIPAL HIGGLEY: We're not exactly sure. I'd still like to get to the bottom of this mystery, but in the meantime it looks like we have you to thank, young man. Are you by any chance available to join our guest of honor onstage at his birthday pep rally this Friday?

PABLO: (*Modestly*) Oh, that's okay. You really don't have to do anything special to thank me.

PRINCIPAL HIGGLEY: No, I insist! We have to do something, as a school, to show our appreciation for your act of good citizenship.

PABLO: Well, if you insist . . .

They exit, talking. Meanwhile, OLIVE enters, looking upset. PEP SQUAD GIRLS #1 and #2 walk by her, gossiping loudly.

PEP SQUAD GIRL #1: Did you hear that Pablo is back on the team?

PEP SQUAD GIRL #2: Get out!

PEP SQUAD GIRL #1: Uh-huh. And did you hear he saved poor Cappy from freezing to death in the park? Pablo's, like, a hero!

PEP SQUAD GIRL #2: Get out!

PEP SQUAD GIRL #1: Uh-huh. And did you hear he did it to impress a girl?

OLIVE: Get out! (*Then, when they do, she realizes that she missed her chance to get key information, so she calls after them.*) No, wait, come back. What team? What girl?!

When they don't return, OLIVE walks over and collapses into a principal's chair next to DEV.

OLIVE (CONT'D): (*To DEV*) I didn't know what to think! Did Pablo lie to me? Was the whole plan concocted to get my attention because he liked me??

DEV: Actually, I think he—

OLIVE: (*Ignoring him*) Or was Pablo just using me? Maybe he was actually trying to impress someone else. Ugh! I'm such an idiot. I believed everything he said: that he liked my creativity, that we'd make a good team, that we were all in this together! (*She does the cheer by herself.*) "One, two, three! Cappy conspiracy!" Dumb, I know. Real dumb. Like that time I thought this guy in my

English class, Bradley Dupree, was interested in me for my wit and charm.

BOY #1 enters, holding a piece of paper.

BOY #1:   Yeah, so, can you write a sonnet for me? And can you make it good, but not too good, okay? Great, and I'll let you know about going to the dance. Though (*fake cough*) I feel like I'm coming down with something, and I wouldn't want to get you sick.

OLIVE: (*Bitterly, to DEV*) I brought him chicken soup. And orange juice. And cough drops. You know who answered the door at his house?

OLIVE rings a doorbell while juggling an armload of supplies. PEP SQUAD GIRL #2 joins BOY #1 and answers the door.

PEP SQUAD GIRL #2:   Omigosh, that looks yummy! But I don't want to fill up too much, because we're getting pizza after the dance. Bradley, how sweet is this random girl from your English class? Adorbs!

OLIVE: (*To DEV*) I may have a blind spot or two when it comes to matters of the heart. So in this case, I needed some answers, fast. I decided to go see the only person who might have them.

DEV: Pablo?

OLIVE: No . . . Brie.

BLACKOUT.

ACT II, SCENE III—FARLEY MIDDLE SCHOOL

Now BRIE is sitting with DEV at the principal's office waiting area, showing him photos on her phone.

BRIE: In Japan, they pretty much worship capybaras. See? They have toys, dolls, clothing, even candy wrapped to look like little capybaras. *(She sighs.)* And look, that's a baby capybara in the wild, just learning the ways of the herd. See how strong and majestic and free he is?

DEV: If you say so.

BRIE: I'm sure it's got to be the oldest story in the book. Girl falls hard and risks everything for love. Looking back, I don't know how I could be so stupid . . . so weak. I don't know how to explain it, except to say . . .

DEV: I get it. You had a thing for Pablo.

BRIE: Pablo? *(She laughs.)* No, not Pablo. Winston. *(She* *sighs happily.)* I'm completely powerless when it comes to capybaras.

BRIE leaves the principal's office waiting-area chairs and takes a seat on a stool in the stables, looking heartbroken. REY joins her, patting her shoulder awkwardly. OLIVE enters and approaches them.

OLIVE: Rey! What are you doing here?

REYNALDO: I'm guessing the same thing as you? Basking in the happy glow of getting called into the principal's office and grilled within an inch of your life?

OLIVE: I know! It was horrible. They told me if they found out I had anything to do with Cappy's disappearance, they'd take away my trip to Florida and get me disqualified from competing in the National Festival of the Performed Word.

REYNALDO: They can't do that! Can they?

OLIVE: I don't know. What'd they threaten you with?

REYNALDO: Detention. Four to six weeks of hard labor, filing in the main office and reshelving in the media center, supervised by the worst drill sergeant you could ask for.

OLIVE: Your mom?

REYNALDO: Yup. And then at some point they told me that Cappy was back and I could leave.

(*Suspiciously*) Which is funny because I thought the plan was for all of us to bring him back and be heroes together. So, Brie and I got to talking. We feel like you have some explaining to do, Olive.

OLIVE: What are you talking about? I didn't bring Cappy back!

REYNALDO: Well, if you didn't and I didn't and Brie didn't, who did?

PABLO walks on, trailed by the PEP SQUAD GIRLS.

PEP SQUAD GIRL #1: Pablo! Hey, Pablo! Wait up!

PEP SQUAD GIRL #2: Yeah, we heard you're, like, a hero.

PEP SQUAD GIRL #1: Not just like a hero. But like a real hero.

PABLO: It was nothing. Listen, girls, I gotta go. Can't miss baseball practice. That's right—I'm back on the team. I'm all about the baseball team! Hoof five!

PEP SQUAD GIRLS #1 and #2:   Hoof five!

The PEP SQUAD GIRLS bump "hooves" with PABLO before he runs off.

PEP SQUAD GIRL #2:   (*Dreamily*) Oh, I am never washing my hoof. I mean hand.

The PEP SQUAD GIRLS exit happily.

OLIVE: Rey, you didn't and I didn't and Brie didn't—it was Pablo! He lied to us. He's not one of us at all. He's a . . . a . . . baseball player!

REYNALDO: I knew it! I guess Pablo was using a different script. A special script he wrote himself, just for him.

OLIVE: Oh, please. He's not a playwright. He's a jock. The only lines he could write are thirty-yard lines.

REYNALDO: Was that a sports joke?

OLIVE: I think so? Was it funny?

REYNALDO: You got me. But I'm not talking about an actual script. I'm talking about the fact that he told us one thing, but the whole time he was using us for a different plan—his plan.

OLIVE: Yeah, for a team player, he's not what you'd call a team player.

BRIE: Wait, Rey, what plan?

OLIVE: (*Ignoring her*) Look, Rey, the point is, if Pablo changed the plan, he did it on his own. I had nothing to do with it.

BRIE: Changed *what* plan?

REYNALDO: (*Ignoring BRIE as well and continuing to argue with OLIVE*) Then how do you explain this ransom note? (*He pulls it out of his pocket and hands it to her.*)

OLIVE: (*Reads it*) You can't seriously suggest I'd be responsible for something this poorly written. I guess Pablo must have planted it to throw suspicion on us instead of him.

REYNALDO: Why, that devious little weasel! That lying little toad—

BRIE: (*Standing on the stool and yelling to get their attention*) HEY! First off, don't take animals' names in vain. Second, I can't believe what I'm hearing. Are you saying that all along you guys have been planning to return Winston to his captors? That this whole thing is some big game to you? That you care nothing about Winston's oppression?

OLIVE and REY exchange guilty looks.

OLIVE: No! I mean, okay, it's true that we weren't aware of the animal-welfare issues at the get-go. But now that we've gotten to know you and Cap—uh, Winston . . .

BRIE: I can't believe I trusted you. And you acted like we were all in this together, even though the whole thing was just a big joke to you. (*Bitterly*) This is the unicorn thing all over.

Several kids enter, whisper, and point at BRIE, then take pencils and put them on their foreheads like unicorn horns before dissolving into laughter and running off.

OLIVE: Brie, it's not like that. We like you, and we admire your dedication to animal rights.

REYNALDO: Yeah. I mean, I'm not entirely convinced that chupacabras should have rights. But if that's your thing, I'm cool with it. From a safe distance, that is.

OLIVE: The reason we agreed to do this in the first place was not to hurt Cappy, or you. The whole point was to show the school that there are lots of kids here who are passionate about activities other than sports.

BRIE: Really?

OLIVE: Really.

REYNALDO: Well, apparently one less than we thought. You know, Pablo. But still, a lot.

OLIVE: I just don't get it. Why would Pablo want to get us involved in taking Cappy in the first place, and then return him without telling us? Why would he do that?

Meanwhile, the PEP SQUAD GIRLS have convinced PABLO to sign autographs for them. They are bending over so he can sign the backs of their shirts.

PEP SQUAD GIRL #1: And make it out to Brendee with three "e's".

PEP SQUAD GIRL #2: (*Jumping up and down*) Ooh, ooh, I want an extra "e," too!

PEP SQUAD GIRL #1: Make that two extra "e's".

PEP SQUAD GIRL #2: (*Jumping up and down*) Three extra "e's"!

PEP SQUAD GIRL #1:   Just keep adding "e's" to our names and don't stop!

REYNALDO: Okay, that could be one reason.

OLIVE: (*Bitterly*) Two reasons.

BRIE: Look, I appreciate that you're trying to help, but the fact remains that because I trusted you, an innocent animal's life is in jeopardy once more. (*Hangs her head*) I am a failure. I'm a total disgrace to P-CUDL.

OLIVE: No, Brie, you're not. You're a really good person with a really big heart. Listen, we'll think of something.

BRIE: Like what? What can you do? Write a big, powerful play that'll make the school administrators see the error in their ways? And get them to apologize and return Winston to the wild? No offense, but last I checked, the principal didn't even know your name.

OLIVE: (*Weakly*) He knows my last name.

BRIE: Face it, Olive. There's nothing you can do about this. There's only one person who can fix this.

PABLO: (*Finishing signing autographs and addressing the PEP SQUAD GIRLS*) You guys will be at the pep rally, right?

The PEP SQUAD GIRLS giggle.

PABLO (CONT'D):   What am I saying? You're on the pep squad. Of course you'll be there. Well, see you there!

He exits.

REYNALDO and OLIVE: (*Looking at each other and saying his name like a curse*) Pablo.

BLACKOUT.

ACT II, SCENE IV—FARLEY MIDDLE SCHOOL

OLIVE is back at the principal's office waiting-area chairs with DEV.

OLIVE: Wednesday morning, Rey and I went to talk to Pablo. As you can imagine, we played it cool.

PABLO is at his locker. OLIVE leaves the chairs, joins REY, and approaches. The two of them are very obviously nervous about the conversation they need to have with PABLO.

OLIVE (CONT'D):   (*To REY*) There he is. Go ahead, I'm right behind you.

REYNALDO: You do it. I can't.

OLIVE: Rey! (*She tries to push REY forward, but when it is obvious he won't be the first to speak, she goes for it.*) Hey, Pablo. Got a minute?

PABLO: (*Without looking at them*) Yeah.

OLIVE and REY rock-paper-scissors over who's going to say it. REY loses.

REYNALDO: (*Frustrated at losing*) Man! Every time? (*He takes a deep breath and makes his approach.*) Pablo, we know what you did.

PABLO: What I did?

OLIVE: (*Gaining momentum as she ticks off items on her fingers*) You lied about not being a jock. You tricked us into helping you kidnap Cappy. And then you returned Cappy without telling us.

REYNALDO: And you planted a ransom note and signed my name!

OLIVE: Yeah! You played the hero while they threatened us with all sorts of punishments. Detention. Filing. Taking away the trip I won.

REYNALDO: Yeah, man, you played us. And now we're going to end up paying for something that wouldn't even have happened if it wasn't for you.

PABLO: Oh, is that so? Funny, from what I recall, "we" didn't need much convincing. You two were the ones talking big about shaking things up and how Che Guevara said . . .

CHE enters, striking an inspiring pose with another apple.

CHE: The revolution is not an apple that falls when it is ripe. You have to . . .

OLIVE: Che? With all due respect, can you give us a minute?

CHE gives her a thumbs-up, takes a bite of the apple, and exits.

OLIVE (CONT'D): Yeah, right, Pablo. I'm the kingpin here, the real crime boss. What do you suppose would happen if Rey and I went to Principal Higgley and told him the truth?

PABLO: Go right ahead. You'd take yourselves down, and you know it. Or maybe you don't. Here's a little lesson I learned from my brother, the jailbird. I fall, you fall. You know what that means.

OLIVE: You're bluffing.

REYNALDO: Your brother's in jail?

PABLO: Want to find out? Go ahead! Go running to Coach K. and Principal Higgley and *your mama.*

He waits while OLIVE and REY look at each other nervously.

PABLO: Yeah, didn't think so. Now listen up. Here's how it's gonna go down. You're gonna keep your mouths shut. Cappy's gonna have his pep rally. I'm gonna be back on my team. And you're gonna go back to your plays and your drama and . . . whatever it is you do.

REYNALDO: You're forgetting one thing. One person, actually, who can't just go back.

BRIE enters, carrying a sign with a picture of CAPPY and a slogan like CAPYBARAS ARE PEOPLE, TOO. *She looks very sad.*

PABLO: Yeah, well, I wouldn't expect you to understand, but I had reasons I did what I did. Some things are more important.

REYNALDO: Like what? *Sports?*

Across the stage, MRS. FUENTES answers the phone.

JAIL RECORDING (VOICE-OVER): You have a call from a correctional institution.

MRS. FUENTES: Luis! *Ay, dios mío,* how are you? You eating okay? How's the arm? Sure, he's here. Pablo, your brother wants to talk to you. Hurry up, they don't give him much time to talk. *(She holds out the phone.)*

LUIS: *(Talking into the phone from his cell)* Bro, when you come to visit next month, can you bring a sewing needle and some thread?

PABLO: *(Nervously)* A "sewing needle"? Is that jailhouse slang for something?

LUIS: You've been watching too many movies, bro. No, a regular old sewing needle. And some thread. My lucky pitching glove sprung a leak, and you can only do so much to fix it with Band-Aids. Look, it's either that or they're gonna send me to the outfield.

PABLO: *(Concerned)* "The outfield"? Is *that* jailhouse slang for something?

LUIS: *(Sarcastically)* Yeah, that's right. "The outfield" is jailhouse slang for . . . the outfield! Left field, right field, center field. I'm a pitcher, you know that. We infielders have our rep to uphold, you know?

They both hang up the phone.

MRS. FUENTES: *(Hovering and peppering Pablo with questions immediately after the two brothers hang up)* Is everything okay? Does he need anything? Is he getting enough to eat?

PABLO: *(To REY, flatly)* Yeah, like sports.

He puts his arm around his mother to comfort her, and together they walk off.

OLIVE: *(To REY)* This isn't over. Oh, no. Far from it.

BLACKOUT.

ACT II, SCENE V—FARLEY MIDDLE SCHOOL

REY is with DEV on the principal's office waiting-area chairs.

REYNALDO: By Thursday, it seemed like the whole Cappy crisis had come and gone. We were back to the same old

Farley Middle School monotony: same kids, same classrooms, same morning announcements.

OLIVE and other students are in homeroom, listening to PRINCIPAL HIGGLEY do the announcements once more. REY leaves DEV to join them.

PRINCIPAL HIGGLEY: Fifty-seven to twelve. Ouch, that's gotta hurt! For the other team, that is. Way to go, Lady Caps! Hoof five, everyone.

The class obeys—hoof bumps all around.

PRINCIPAL HIGGLEY (CONT'D): Now remember, tomorrow is a big day for our marvelous mascot, Cappy the Capybara. He's turning five, so we'll have a special pep rally in his honor, with an extra-special guest, Pablo Fuentes, better known as the member of our baseball team who rescued Cappy all by himself and returned him safe and sound!

REYNALDO: *(To OLIVE)* I can't believe I'm saying this, but now that Pablo gave the chupacabra back, life is back to the same old same old.

PABLO storms into homeroom angrily.

PABLO: *(To REY)* Okay, what did you do with him?

REYNALDO: Do with who?

PABLO: Don't play dumb. You know who I mean. (*Looks around secretively, then whispers*) Cappy. What did you do with Cappy?

OLIVE: Last I checked, *you* were the one who did something with Cappy. What was it again? Oh, I know! You traded his freedom for a pack of baseball cards.

REYNALDO: After you tricked us into helping you take him in the first place. A little fact you neglected to reveal when you returned the stolen merchandise.

PABLO: Hey, it wasn't like that!

REYNALDO: Oh yeah? What was it like?

PABLO: Well . . .

We proceed to see what it was like. PRINCIPAL HIGGLEY and MRS. DELGADO enter and fawn all over PABLO at one side while OLIVE and REY watch in disgust.

PRINCIPAL HIGGLEY: There he is! Pablo, we are so grateful to you for rescuing our beloved mascot and saving our entire school's spirit. It is amazing that one student did this all by himself.

PABLO: Yeah, um, I guess so.

MRS. DELGADO: Oh, and he's modest, too! I wish my son Reynaldo were more like you. Thinking of others instead of spending hours in the bathroom staring at himself in the mirror. Or whatever else it is he does in there.

REYNALDO: (*Embarrassed*) Mom! It's not like that. I'm just very hygienic!

PRINCIPAL HIGGLEY: Anything you want, Pablo, just ask. You've earned it, son! All by yourself.

PABLO: Well, ordinarily, I'd ask for something special— not for myself but for my teammates. You know, on the baseball team. Except coach says that, with my grades, I can't be on the baseball team anymore.

PRINCIPAL HIGGLEY: Really? Well, that's a shame, with that arm of yours. (*He pulls a ball out of his pocket and tosses it to PABLO, who sends it back.*)

MRS. DELGADO: We have tutoring sessions in the media center after school. I'm sure with some extra support and studying, those grades would go up in no time.

PRINCIPAL HIGGLEY: See? It's as easy as that. Meanwhile, I'll have a little talk with Coach K. about reinstating you to the team while you work on kicking your report card's butt! It's the least we can do for the student athlete who returned our missing mascot and saved our school from a plummeting pep problem. And speaking of pep, we've got a pep rally in your honor to plan! Mrs. D., can you call in an order for those hoof-shaped cookies we get for special occasions?

MRS. DELGADO: The frosted ones? I'm on it.

PRINCIPAL HIGGLEY: And we'll also need to order more balloons and rent a trampoline for the pep squad and . . .

PABLO: Oh, and there is one other thing . . .

But MRS. DELGADO and PRINCIPAL HIGGLEY have already walked off, continuing to plan.

PABLO (CONT'D): (*Calling after them*) The drama club would like to use the auditorium sometimes. . . .

OLIVE: (*Perks up*) Really? You asked them about that? What did they say?

REYNALDO: Olive! Wake up! He's lying to us again.

PABLO: That's not true! I really did ask. I mean, I would have asked, except they were so busy planning the pep rally. But anyway, I'm not lying about Cappy! This time, Cappy is gone. *Really* gone!

REYNALDO: Like . . . ? (*Makes gagging noise and mimes slitting his own throat*)

PABLO: Dunno. But he's definitely missing again.

OLIVE: That's not possible. You already brought him back. And you heard Principal Higgley. They're planning his welcome-back birthday bonanza, which is tomorrow!

PABLO: Well, it might have to be a going-away party. Cappy is AWOL. Coach K. hasn't even told Principal Higgley. I think he's afraid he might get fired for losing the mascot twice!

REYNALDO: Are you trying to suggest that we would take him again? After everything we went through the first time and the punishments they've threatened? How dumb do you think we are?

PABLO: Well, who else would do it?

BRIE walks onstage, talking privately on her cell phone.

BRIE: Hello?! Ugh, menu.

CAPYBARA LIBERATION FRONT (VOICE-OVER): Thank you for calling the Capybara Liberation Front. Please listen to the following options, as our menu has changed. *Para español, oprima número dos.* If you're calling to report a capybara emergency, please hang up and dial 911 or go to the nearest twenty-four-hour exotic veterinary practice. If you'd like to report an incident of capybara abuse, press seven. If you've kidnapped your school mascot for the second time and don't want your friends to know it was you, press nine.

BRIE presses the button.

OLIVE: (*To REY and PABLO*) No way. She may be crazy, but she's not that crazy.

REYNALDO: She might be. I read that if a chupacabra sucks a little of your blood but not, like, all of it, you could become part chupacabra yourself. Which could explain a lot of this.

OLIVE: Rey! You have got to stay off the Internet.

PABLO: All I can say is, if I get kicked off the baseball team again, somebody's gonna pay.

The bell rings and OLIVE, REYNALDO, and PABLO head out of class. PABLO storms off as REY and OLIVE approach BRIE.

BRIE: (*Hanging up the phone quickly*) Oh hey, guys, what's up?

REYNALDO: Nothing. No, nope, nothing at all. *(He holds his neck, as if afraid she's going to bite him.)*

BRIE: What's wrong with your neck? And what were you doing with Pablo?

OLIVE: Pablo was just telling us the latest about Cappy.

BRIE: Oh yeah? What are they going to do, shoot him out of a cannon at the big pep rally?

Across the stage, PRINCIPAL HIGGLEY and MRS. DELGADO enter, still in party-planning mode. At the sound of the word "cannon," PRINCIPAL HIGGLEY is struck by inspiration.

PRINCIPAL HIGGLEY: That's it! For the finale, we can shoot Cappy out of a cannon.

MRS. DELGADO: Love it!

MRS. DELGADO scribbles notes on her pad as they walk off.

BRIE: *(Calling out in their direction)* I was being facetious!

OLIVE: Pablo says Cappy's missing again. You know anything about that?

BRIE: He's what?! That's awful! He could be lost in the wilds of suburban Maryland. Cold. Hungry. Unless . . . you don't suppose the Capybara Liberation Front is somehow involved?

OLIVE: Brie, I know this might be hard for you to accept, but there is no Capybara Liberation Front! There is no one championing the rights of capybaras at this school except you.

BRIE: That's not true. I'll have you know that P-CUDL has several registered members at Farley Middle School.

OLIVE: Several?

BRIE: Yes! Okay, fine, maybe not dues-paying members, but I had a very successful bake sale recently, and lots of kids took pamphlets.

REYNALDO: Ohhhh! I remember that! Those red velvet cupcakes were incredible.

BRIE: Thanks! They were vegan, too.

REYNALDO: No kidding?

BRIE: Yeah, I can give you the recipe. (*Realizing that she's moved off topic and shifting back to being outraged*) The point is, if I did rescue Winston this time—which I did

NOT—I'd have him in a safe house by now. They'd never find him and never bring him back to his life of oppression and slavery and (*pointed look in the direction where PRINCIPAL HIGGLEY and Mrs. DELGADO exited*) cannons.

OLIVE: In other words, if you took him, you'd never admit it.

BRIE: Precisely. But I didn't!

OLIVE: But you do know where he might go or what he might do, if he got loose?

REYNALDO: We could call the Red Cross and see if anyone hairy and big-nosed tried to make a bloodbank withdrawal?

BRIE: Of course I know where he might go. I'm an expert on capybaras. But why should I help you guys? The last time I trusted you, Winston ended up back with his captors.

OLIVE: That wasn't us, Brie. That was Pablo!

BRIE: Olive, just admit it. If Pablo hadn't beaten you to it, I think we both know what would've happened. . . . I can picture it now.

OLIVE: Oh yeah? Well, believe me, I can picture it, too. . . .

They look off to one side, where PRINCIPAL HIGGLEY and MRS. DELGADO enter. OLIVE joins them.

PRINCIPAL HIGGLEY: Young lady, thank you SO much for bringing back our Cappy! I wish there was something our school could do to show our gratitude to you, uh . . .

OLIVE: Olive. It's Olive. Olive Henry.

PRINCIPAL HIGGLEY: Right! Right, the girl named Henry! You . . . write things?

OLIVE: Close enough. Yes, I do. I write plays, and I was hoping I could have a chance to hold some rehearsals in the auditorium. You know, the big room with the stage?

PRINCIPAL HIGGLEY: You mean where the Frisbee club practices?

OLIVE: Yes.

PRINCIPAL HIGGLEY: Well, uh, sure. I mean, without you and only you, we wouldn't have our beloved school mascot back.

REYNALDO: (*From across the stage, clearing his throat*) Ahem?

PRINCIPAL HIGGLEY: You're our hero, Olive Henry.

OLIVE basks in the moment a few more beats.

REYNALDO: (*From across the stage, clearing his throat even more loudly*) Ah-h-h-hem?

OLIVE: Oh, actually, it wasn't just me. My friends also helped a lot.

CHE enters, holding up an apple and clearing his throat even more loudly than REY did.

CHE: Ah-h-h-HEM!

OLIVE: (*Finally taking the hint*) And we did it for a reason. To achieve liberty and justice for all kids at this school, not just the ones who are good at sports.

PRINCIPAL HIGGLEY: Olive, I may not be a writer, but I've seen enough movies to know a thing or two. In a buddy comedy, it's fine to have two guys tussling over the spotlight. But in a hero's journey, there's only one hero.

OLIVE: Yes, but you see—

PRINCIPAL HIGGLEY: You're that hero, Henry. You've earned it, just like that Super Bowl–of–scripting trophy you're going to win. Claim what is yours! Moments like this don't come along every day. Blink and you'll miss it.

CHE exits, shaking his head in disbelief. OLIVE backs away, drifting back to REY and BRIE as PRINCIPAL HIGGLEY exits.

OLIVE: (*Dreamily*) I won't blink. I won't blink. I won't blink.

REYNALDO: Brie, the bottom line is that if Principal Higgley discovers Cappy is missing again, he's going to reopen the investigation. And then we'll all be in hot water.

BRIE: Not to mention there's a vulnerable animal out there, lost, maybe hurt, with potential danger at every turn.

OLIVE: And they say I'm dramatic. Look, lunch period's about to start. Let's split up and search. Rey, you recheck Coach K.'s office, the ball fields, and the bushes behind school. Brie, you check out all bodies of water in the vicinity, large and small. I'm talking public fountains as well as ponds—anything Cappy might see as useful if nature called. You guys text me if you need emergency backup. Otherwise, we'll meet back here in forty-five minutes.

BRIE nods and exits.

REYNALDO: Wait, what's your assignment?

OLIVE: (*Looking around to make sure the coast is clear*) Come with me. I have a hunch, and there's not a moment to waste.

OLIVE and REY run off.

ACT III, SCENE I—FARLEY MIDDLE SCHOOL

DEV and REY are sitting in the chairs outside the principal's office.

REYNALDO: (*To DEV*) Honestly, I was starting to feel like I was the only one who was not going crazy. We've got Cappy—we don't have Cappy—Coach K.'s got Cappy—Coach K. doesn't have Cappy. And then Olive started acting so weird. But once Olive's hunch proved correct, I knew I needed to get to Brie quickly . . . before someone else did.

REY walks to the Farley Middle School boys' restroom and dials his cell phone. BRIE wanders onstage nearby, and her phone rings. She checks to see who is calling, looks surprised, and answers.

BRIE: (*Into her phone*) Rey? What's up? Everything okay? Did you find him? Where are you?

REYNALDO: I just got back from looking, and I'm actually calling you from the boys' room at school. Thing is, I kind of need to keep this on the down low. Olive can't know I told you.

Long pause.

BRIE: Told me what?

REYNALDO: About Cappy. I mean Whatever-You-Call-Him. We know that you've got him.

BRIE: (*Nervously*) I don't know what you're talking about. I'm looking for him in fountains and puddles, like Olive said. No luck yet.

REYNALDO: Brie, we went by your house.

BRIE: Oh?

REYNALDO: We saw him, Brie. We saw him there in the stables just now, me and Olive.

BRIE: Are you sure you didn't just see my guinea pigs? There's a whole lot of them, and when they fall asleep together in a pile, it might kind of look like . . .

REYNALDO: Brie! It was not thirteen little chupacabras;

it was one big one. Plus all the little ones, too, obviously, but that's not the point. How could you take him again? What were you thinking? I know you care about him. But come on!

BRIE: It's not just that I care about him, Rey. I connect with him on a deeper level. Capybaras are my spirit animal. I'm not sure if it's their gentle eyes or their big sweet snouts or their superior intelligence, but—

REYNALDO: Listen to me. I am *not* a capybara enthusiast. Cappy smells like dirty socks, and I'll bet you a dollar he's going to suck out all your blood while you're asleep. I know I was dumb enough to get involved with taking him once, but I can't believe anyone would be dumb enough to do it again.

BRIE: (*Flatly*) Don't hold back. Tell me what you really think. I can take it.

REYNALDO: I'm sorry. I didn't call to yell at you. I called to warn you.

BRIE: Warn me? About what? Is Olive going to take him back to captivity?

REYNALDO: No way. I mean, sure, Olive thinks you're nuts for taking Cappy again—and she'd definitely think

I am, too, if she knew I was helping you—but she's not going to stand in your way. I'm just afraid that someone else might.

BRIE: You're talking about Pablo? He doesn't know. And he doesn't have to know!

PEP SQUAD GIRLS #1 and #2 walk past BRIE, lost in conversation.

PEP SQUAD GIRL #1: So I heard that she said that he said that she said she knew what he said.

PEP SQUAD GIRL #2: Oh yeah? Well, I heard that she told her that he said that she also told her that—

REYNALDO: (*To BRIE*) Right, because news just doesn't travel at this school.

BRIE: Well, fine. So what if Pablo does find out? By then it'll be too late. I will have transported him to an animal sanctuary.

REYNALDO: I'm not talking about Cappy's well-being. Brie, I don't know if you're aware of this, but Pablo's kind of . . .

BRIE: Cute?

REYNALDO: You too? Olive's the same way about him. I'm not talking about cute; though, yes, he is. I'm talking about intense. It kind of worries me. It's like he'll stop at nothing to find Cappy and bring him back.

BRIE: What makes you say that?

REYNALDO: Let's just say I'm a guy. I hear stuff.

Two BOYS walk into the bathroom, talking.

BOY #1: And then he said, *Oh yeah?* And he was like, *Yeah, you wanna make something of it?*

BOY #2: Nah, man, that's not how it went down. He was all—(*the rest of the conversation is explained in gestures*) And he was like (*gesture*), and the next thing, *bam!* (*More gestures of fighting*)

REYNALDO: (*To BRIE*) I don't always understand it, but I definitely hear it. Did you know Pablo (*whispers into the phone*) has a brother in jail?

BOY #1: (*Who has been eavesdropping, to REY*) Yo, I heard that, too.

BOY #2: Heard what?

BOY #1: That this kid Pablo, who used to be on the baseball team, has a brother who—

REYNALDO: *(To BOYS)* Can you give us a minute here?

Both BOYS put hands up, like "sorry," while REY turns away.

BRIE: You think Pablo is going to help his brother break out of jail so they can come after me?

REYNALDO: Maybe? I mean, I don't know. I just don't want to see you get hurt. I think you're in way over your head with this whole chupacabra business.

BRIE: *Capybara.* And that's really sweet, Rey, but it's a risk I'm going to have to take. I swore I would rescue Winston from his oppression, no matter what it took. But, since you're offering . . .

REYNALDO: Wait, hang on, I'm not—

BRIE: You can help me get Winston to safety! Once I figure out how, that is. I can't get through to an actual human being at the Capybara Liberation Front. I keep getting their stupid voice mail! Okay, think, think . . . I've got it! No . . .

REYNALDO: What about . . . No, that won't work. He

probably wouldn't survive being mailed internationally, even with air holes.

BRIE: Hey, I've got an idea! You can't tell Olive, though. If she's got a crush on Pablo, that could put Winston at risk. Can your mom give us a ride to the National Zoo after school today?

REYNALDO: I have no idea. Maybe? Why?

BRIE: I'll explain later. Pick me up at my house at four o'clock. Oh, and Rey? Tell your mom we're taking my little sister.

REYNALDO: You have a little sister?

BRIE: Not exactly. But tell her I do, okay? Oh, and I should probably borrow a car seat if we're going to make this believable. My next-door neighbor might have one—I'll go ask. Gotta go. See you soon! *(She hangs up.)*

BRIE runs off.

REYNALDO: Car seat? Zoo? Hello? *(Hanging up)* I've got a bad feeling about this.

BLACKOUT.

ACT III, SCENE II—FARLEY MIDDLE SCHOOL

OLIVE is now with DEV at the principal's office waiting-area chairs.

OLIVE: So, meanwhile, I was trying to figure out why Rey was acting so weird. First, when we got to Brie's and Rey saw for himself that my hunch was right and she was the one who stole Cappy back, he left in a hurry without saying anything. And when I got back to school, he seemed really nervous, though he said everything was fine. And then, when I went to meet him at our lockers after school, like we do every day, he wasn't there. I had to look all over for him.

MRS. DELGADO is at her desk. REY enters and approaches her.

REYNALDO: Mom? You ready? Can we go? Now?

MRS. DELGADO: Relax, Rey. I've never seen you so jumpy, and that's saying a lot. The zoo is not going to close before we get there. So just calm down and let me get my purse.

OLIVE leaves DEV and goes to talk to REY.

OLIVE: Hey, Mrs. D. Have you seen—(*sees REY*) Rey, where have you been?! I need to talk with you about *(pointedly, using the words as code for something else) the script I wrote,* you know the one.

MRS. DELGADO: Well, hello, Olive. Are you coming with us to the zoo?

OLIVE: The zoo? *(To REY) You're* going to the zoo?

REYNALDO: *(Laughing)* Yeah, you know me. Can't get enough of the zoo.

MRS. DELGADO: I told Rey I'd give you two a ride. Are you ready to go?

REYNALDO: Mom, I said me and a friend, but I meant a different friend. Sorry, Olive.

MRS. DELGADO: That's okay. We have room for you, too, Olive. If you'd like to come.

REYNALDO: Nah, Mom. We don't have room. My friend's bringing her little sister, remember? And her car seat?

MRS. DELGADO: *(Looking at him like he's crazy)* I drive a minivan, Rey. Trust me, even with a car seat, we'll have room. It's fine with me, Olive. The more, the merrier.

OLIVE: Thanks, Mrs. D. Actually, the zoo sounds like a lot of fun. Don't mind if I do.

They walk to the car. MRS. DELGADO gets in front, and REY and OLIVE sit behind her.

REYNALDO: (*Whispering*) Okay, listen, when we pick her up, you might be kind of mad, but I can explain. It's for a good reason.

OLIVE: (*Also whispering*) What are you talking about?

They pull up at BRIE's house. She is pushing a baby stroller, loaded up with a large bundle wearing sunglasses and a bucket hat. Under her arm is a booster-style car seat.

BRIE: Thanks for picking me u— Oh! (*Nervously*) Hi, Olive.

REYNALDO: (*To OLIVE*) Don't be mad. I can explain. (*Whispering*) Please play along!

OLIVE: (*Playing along as best she can*) Ohhhh, hi, Brie! Nice day for a trip to the zoo, huh? Is this your sister? I didn't know you had a sister.

BRIE: Yup, I do. But she's having her nap, so whatever you do, DON'T disturb her.

OLIVE: Is she wearing little furry booties? That is so cute! I used to have—(*it suddenly dawns on her*) Wait a second. . . . Are you trying to tell me—

REY and BRIE shake their heads as if to say "no, of course not" when they actually mean "please don't blow it!"

OLIVE (CONT'D): Wow, your sister, huh? I'll bet she's pretty hairy. I mean she has pretty hair! What's her name?

BRIE: Win—(*catches herself*) Winnie.

BRIE puts the car seat on a seat at the back of the mini-van and then transfers the bundle to it before sitting in the seat next to it. OLIVE and REY sit in the middle row, behind MRS. DELGADO, who is driving.

REYNALDO: Okay, be sure to get Winnie all buckled up. My mom is a bug about safety. Aren't you, Mom?

MRS. DELGADO: You've got that right. Is everybody buckled?

All ad-lib in the affirmative.

MRS. DELGADO (CONT'D): Okay, here we go. This really takes me back, Rey. When you and your sisters were little, we used to go to the zoo all the time. Remember how you used to like to sing songs on the drive there?

REYNALDO: Mom!!!

MRS. DELGADO: (*Ignoring him*) Your favorite one was . . . (*sings*) "The wheels on the bus go round and round, round and round, round and round . . ."

OLIVE *and* BRIE *laugh and join in, while* REY *cringes in embarrassment.*

MRS. DELGADO, BRIE, and OLIVE: "The wheels on the bus go round and round, all through the town."

MRS. DELGADO: "The wipers on the bus go . . ."

CAPPY: (*Coming out from under the sheet*) Wheek! Wheek! Wheek!

MRS. DELGADO: (*Looking up, startled*) What was that?

REYNALDO: (*Quickly trying to divert attention*) Wait, no! Now I remember. It's not "wheek, wheek, wheek." They go "swish, swish, swish." (*He does wiper-arm movements quickly to distract his mom.*) Right, Mom?

MRS. DELGADO: All together now!

BRIE *quickly attends to* CAPPY *and gets him covered up again.* REY *and* OLIVE *obey, singing "swish, swish, swish" and waving their arms like wipers.* MRS. DELGADO *pulls up at the zoo and turns around in her seat. There are* NATIONAL ZOO *signs with ar-*

rows pointing to GIANT PANDAS *and* SMALL MAMMAL HOUSE, *etc.*

MRS. DELGADO (CONT'D): Well, that was fun. Okay, kids, here we are at the National Zoo. I'll pick you guys up in an hour. All right?

REYNALDO: Got it. Thanks, Mom.

MRS. DELGADO: Have a good time! *Ahhh* . . . Starbucks, here I come.

She waves and drives off.

OLIVE: Okay, what is going on? Why do you have Cappy again, and why are you taking him to the zoo—

REYNALDO: Well, we offered to take him to the circus, but apparently he's afraid of clowns. Ba-dum-tss! *(He waits a beat.)* Just kidding. Sorry . . . couldn't resist.

BRIE: Rey, come on, this is no time for jokes. Look, Olive, Rey and I have talked, and we both agree that he can't go back to his captors. He needs to be properly cared for, have opportunities to socialize with his own kind, maybe even find a mate.

OLIVE: So, let me get this straight. . . . You put all of us at risk to help the world's largest rodent get a date?

REYNALDO: Olive, it's more complicated than that. Just listen to her, will you?

OLIVE: No, I won't! This has gone too far, Rey. We made a bad decision once, and we were lucky enough to get away with it. I don't want to go down that road again!

REYNALDO: What about liberty and justice for all kids, not just the ones who play sports? Have you forgotten about that?

OLIVE: Of course not! But, Rey, they're going to take away my trip. I for one want the liberty and justice to go to Florida.

REYNALDO: Oh, okay. I get it. This is all about you. And here I thought you and Pablo didn't have anything in common.

OLIVE: Rey, don't be like that. You know that's not the only reason! I mean, come on, who are we kidding? If things had gone as planned and they actually paid attention to our demands, that would have lasted for, what, fifteen minutes? And then it would've gone right back to business as usual. Face it, Rey: we have no voice.

BRIE: Capybaras have no voice, which is why I began to speak up for them in the first place.

REYNALDO: Speaking of capybaras, now that we're here at the zoo, shouldn't we, you know . . .

BRIE: "Young people, when informed and empowered, when they realize that what they do truly makes a difference, can indeed change the world." Jane Goodall said that. She first went to Africa when she was twenty-three. She hadn't even gone to college yet. And she went on to make history.

OLIVE: Really? Did Jane Goodall make history by kidnapping a capybara? Twice?! I don't think so!

REYNALDO: Look, Olive. Every time we do a play, we do things your way. You write, you direct, you cast all the parts. You don't just write the programs—you write the reviews!

OLIVE: (*Miffed*) You write some of the reviews. I just massage them a little to give them that extra oomph.

REYNALDO: Just this once, let someone else be the leader. It won't hurt you, I promise.

BRIE: Not only that, it will keep Winston from being hurt any more, and that's what really matters. The plan is pretty simple: we're going to put him into a habitat here. Without anyone seeing us, of course.

REYNALDO: Okay, well, there's no reason for you to know this, but stipulation number three was that I don't touch him. So I can stand lookout if you two want to go ahead.

BRIE: Rey! He's heavy—I can't lift him over the barriers myself. Plus, he's harmless! Especially since he's knocked out at the moment.

OLIVE: Knocked out?

She looks in the stroller more carefully.

OLIVE (CONT'D): Omigosh, he was squawking up a storm in the car, but now he's out cold. What did you do to him?

BRIE: It's nothing. Just a little Benadryl. I give it to my guinea pigs whenever they have to go for vet visits. Totally mellows them out.

OLIVE: Brie, have you lost your mind? You kidnapped Cappy a second time, drugged him, and now you're dumping him at the zoo. Plus, are there even any capybaras in this exhibit? The sign says "Collared Peccaries."

BRIE: His name is Winston! And they used to have capybaras here, but not anymore. If you knew anything at all about capybaras, you would know that capybaras and collared peccaries can live in the same habitat. Look, the bottom line is that the zoo handlers will notice him immediately. Once they've checked him out, they'll transfer him to a sanctuary where he can join a herd and enjoy the life he's supposed to have. Okay? It's really the best thing for him. So can you give me a hand lifting him into the habitat before he wakes up?

OLIVE: No, Brie! We need to get him back to school before anyone finds out that you took him again. Rey, come on! You're my best friend. You're supposed to take my side no matter what.

REYNALDO: Olive . . .

BRIE: Rey . . .

OLIVE: Brie . . .

Unbeknownst to them, a figure is lurking nearby.

PABLO: Too late.

OLIVE, REY, and BRIE: Pablo!

He closes in on them as they try to hide the stroller and hold him off.

OLIVE: Pablo! Hey! Uh, what brings you to the zoo? Didn't know you were such an animal lover.

PABLO: I'm here about a specific animal. A capybara. Know anything about that?

OLIVE: Well, it's the world's largest rodent. Originally from South America but very popular in Japan. Likes to do its business underwater . . .

REYNALDO: Yeah, funny thing about capybaras. They used to have them here at the zoo, and then a few years ago they changed the exhibits, so—

PABLO: Don't play games. I know you have him. Hand him over, and nobody gets hurt.

BRIE: If you want to get to him, you'll have to get through me first. I will defend Winston's freedom and well-being by any means necessary.

PABLO: Have it your way.

PABLO reaches out to grab the stroller.

BRIE: No, you can't! I won't let you!

She lunges for the stroller and a tug-of-war between BRIE and PABLO ensues.

OLIVE: (*To REY*) What are we going to do? Shouldn't the zoo have, like, zoo cops or something?

PABLO: You're—making—a—big—mistake—

REYNALDO: We've got to get help.

They rock-paper-scissors for it. REY throws scissors and loses to OLIVE's rock.

REYNALDO (CONT'D): (*Disappointed to lose once again*) Man! Knew I shoulda gone with paper.

OLIVE: I'll be right back!

She dashes off.

BRIE: I know aikido! Stand back! Hi-YAH!

With one well-aimed motion, BRIE flips PABLO to the ground and knocks him out cold.

REYNALDO: Omigosh! What did you do, Brie?

BRIE: A little move I call "the Benadryl."

REYNALDO: Good name. He's out cold.

BRIE: Quick, let's get Winston in and get out of here before Pablo wakes up.

REYNALDO: Right, but I don't— Oh, all right, fine. I can't believe I'm doing this. . . .

REY pulls his sleeves down over his hands, reaches into the stroller, and lifts CAPPY out, depositing him over the wa—

BRIE: Wait! I . . . I need a moment.

REYNALDO: Okay, but quickly. He's heavy! And he could wake up any minute! And so could Pablo!!

BRIE: Hey there, Winston. I just want you to know that I'm really going to miss you. I know we were only together a short time, and then not, and then again for a short time, but the point is, you're really special to me. I don't know if I'm ever going to see you again, because they'll probably ship you to a sanctuary in Japan, or somewhere else where capybaras are worshipped as they should be, but that's okay. Because whenever I think about you, I'll know that you're happy and that you're running around and swimming and maybe even having a family and doing all those things capybaras are supposed to do. I'll know that you're not getting blasted out of a cannon or hoisted to the top of a pyramid or anything like that. I'll know that you're free to live the capybara life that you want, the one you deserve.

REYNALDO: Arms. Losing feeling in my arms.

BRIE: You're lucky, Winston. But you know what? I'm lucky, too. If it hadn't been for you, I wouldn't have met Rey, who's, like, the first person that ever went out on a limb for me. I didn't think friendship like that existed in the human world. Rey says he doesn't care about you, but I think we both know he's just hiding his feelings so no one will see his tender side.

REYNALDO: Not even close. Also, please wrap it up.

BRIE: And Olive. I guess I can't blame her. She's worked hard writing plays, and she deserves her happiness every bit as much as you do. Besides, if she hadn't wanted to shake our school up so badly, we never would have taken you in the first place. And I wouldn't be here today, so close to giving you your first taste of freedom. . . . It's all worth it to give you your . . .

I can't do it.

REYNALDO: What? Can't do what?

BRIE: This. Rey, I can't let him go. I'm sorry! I know the right thing to do would be to give him a life he deserves. But . . . I deserve happiness, too. And the past week, I've been happier than I've ever been before. That's why I took him again in the first place. I missed him. I guess I'm no better than his captors, huh?

REYNALDO: Brie, don't you know that saying? They put it on T-shirts? Something about "If you love something, set it free"? You love him, I get it, but you can't hold on . . . or actually I can't hold on . . . any longer. . . .

REY starts to deposit CAPPY into the enclosure.

LOUD, MENACING VOICE (OFFSTAGE): FREEZE! NOBODY MOVE A MUSCLE.

REYNALDO: Omigosh, it's Pablo's brother! We're all gonna die!

PABLO stirs. REY keeps holding CAPPY in his arms.

PABLO: (*Sleepily*) What'd you say about my brother?

REYNALDO: What? Oh, I just said, "Heyyyyy! Pablo! My brother!"

PABLO: (*Confused*) You're not my brother. My brother's name is Luis. Your name is . . .

REYNALDO: No, I mean, not literally. I just meant, you know, like "hey, brother!"

PABLO: My head hurts. Did I get hit with a baseball?

REYNALDO: Yes. That's exactly what happened.

LOUD, MENACING VOICE (OFFSTAGE): I SAID FREEZE! NOBODY MOVE A MUSCLE.

REYNALDO: Aaaugghhh!!! Pablo's brother! We're all gonna die!

PABLO: Why do you keep saying that? My brother, Luis, is locked up. He's not coming home for a long, looooong time.

REYNALDO: I'm sorry.

PABLO: Thanks. It's been really hard on me and my mom.

REYNALDO: Yeah, that sounds pretty rough. I can't even imagine. But, hey, if that loud, menacing voice isn't your brother, who is it?

LOUD, MENACING VOICE (OFFSTAGE): LOWER THE CAPYBARA. GENTLY. AND BACK AWAY FROM IT. NOW.

REYNALDO: I'm lowering! I'm backing! Don't shoot!

He places CAPPY on the ground and puts his hands in the air.

LOUD, MENACING VOICE (OFFSTAGE): YOUNG MAN, YOU ARE IN BIG TROUBLE.

REYNALDO: (*Incredulous*) Mom???

MRS. DELGADO strides onstage and strikes a pose, hands on hips. OLIVE follows on her heels.

MRS. DELGADO: (*Proudly*) That's right, I'm with the Capybara Liberation Front. Middle school administrator–slash–media specialist by day, animal-rights activist by night.

OLIVE: (*To audience*) Right? Just when you thought Mrs. D. couldn't get any cooler!

BRIE: Wait, the Capybara Liberation Front is you? I can't believe it. How come you haven't been returning my calls?

MRS. DELGADO: Please. I work in the main office of a public school, and I'm the school media specialist in my so-called free time. Do you have any idea how little time I have to make personal calls? Not to mention I have three children, (*pointedly*) one of whom requires a fairly large amount of attention.

REYNALDO: (*Guiltily*) Love you, Mom.

MRS. DELGADO: (*Curtly*) We'll talk later. Now, where's the capybara. You put him in the habitat?

REYNALDO: No. You said to lower him and back away. I put him on the ground right there by the sign.

Everyone realizes what has happened.

ALL EXCEPT PABLO: (*Ad-lib, calling out as they scatter to look for him*) Cappy! Winston! Here, boy! Here, Cappy Cappy Cappy Cappy! Win-STON!

PABLO: I don't feel so good.

He lies down again. BLACKOUT.

ACT III, SCENE III—FARLEY MIDDLE SCHOOL

OLIVE and DEV are in the principal's office waiting-area chairs.

DEV: So, that's it? What happened to Cappy?

OLIVE: Cappy's in a much better place now.

DEV: That's terrible.

OLIVE: No, it's really for the best. The situation reached its crescendo at Friday's pep rally, which, as you heard, was supposed to be a big birthday party for Cappy.

At the pep rally, signs say CAPPY BIRTHDAY! *and* CAP-TASTIC CAPPY! *and similar. There are balloons, crepe paper, etc. And of course the PEP SQUAD is working the crowd. PRINCIPAL HIGGLEY and COACH K. stand by, at the microphone stand or podium, admiring the scene. REY and BRIE are present as well, with the other students.*

PEP SQUAD GIRL #1:   Two, four, six, eight! Capybaras, lookin' great!

PEP SQUAD GIRL #2:   Eight, six, four, two! Cappy spirit, how 'bout you?

PEP SQUAD GIRL #1:   We say Cappy! You say birthday!

PEP SQUAD GIRL #2:   CAPPY!

PEP SQUAD GIRL #1:   (*Encouraging the crowd*) BIRTHDAY!

PEP SQUAD GIRL #2:   CAPPY!

PEP SQUAD GIRL #1: BIRTHDAY!

PRINCIPAL HIGGLEY: (*To COACH K.*) Ah, what a glorious day for a pep rally, wouldn't you say? And where's our guest of honor?

COACH K.: That Fuentes kid must have him. You know, Pablo Fuentes? Said he was taking Cappy out to get him washed and groomed.

PRINCIPAL HIGGLEY: Does one do that? Groom capybaras?

COACH K.: Occasionally.

PRINCIPAL HIGGLEY: How much does it cost to have a capybara groomed?

Before he can answer, MRS. DELGADO enters and beckons to OLIVE. OLIVE leaves the principal's office waiting-area chairs to join her, and together they approach COACH K.

MRS. DELGADO: Coach K.? Can we have a word with you?

COACH K.: Sure.

They walk to one side and huddle in private conversation. Meanwhile, the PEP SQUAD is at it again.

PEP SQUAD GIRL #1:   We say Cappy! You say love ya!

PEP SQUAD GIRL #2:   CAPPY!

PEP SQUAD GIRL #1:   (*Encouraging the crowd*) LOVE YA!

PEP SQUAD GIRL #2:   CAPPY!

PEP SQUAD GIRL #1:   LOVE YA!

PEP SQUAD GIRLS: WOOOOO! YEAH!!! (*Jumping up and down with their pom-poms, doing splits, etc.*)

COACH K. returns to PRINCIPAL HIGGLEY, sticking a wad of cash in his pocket as he walks.

COACH K.:   We're all set. Ready to start the show.

PRINCIPAL HIGGLEY: Well, it's about time. Mrs. Delgado, can you do the honors?

MRS. DELGADO: No worries, chief. I got this.

She takes the microphone and addresses the audience.

MRS. DELGADO (CONT'D):   Boys and girls, faculty and staff, it is my great honor to introduce to you someone who is a true friend of our beloved Cappy. Ladies and gentlemen, Olive Henry!

PRINCIPAL HIGGLEY: Who?

OLIVE: Thank you, Mrs. Delgado. Fellow students, teachers, Principal Higgley. You're probably wondering why I'm up here today, and that's fair. This is a pep rally for Cappy, not for me. (*Deep breath*)

I am here to tell you that Cappy's not here. And he's not coming back. And that's because . . . I kidnapped Cappy.

There is a gasp from the crowd and exaggerated gasps from the PEP SQUAD.

OLIVE (CONT'D):   Yup, I took him. I'm not trying to make excuses, though I do have a good reason, which I'll get to in a—

PABLO, who has been at the back of the crowd, suddenly runs up to the podium.

PABLO: Olive, stop. I can't let you do this. Listen up, she's just taking the rap for me. It was me. I kidnapped Cappy.

There is another gasp from the crowd and exaggerated gasps from the PEP SQUAD.

PABLO (CONT'D):   It's true. I did it to make it look like I'm a hero so they'd put me back on the baseball team.

Which they kicked me off of on account of my grades. And probably my attitude.

COACH K. nods in agreement.

PABLO: I'm no hero. I put what I wanted ahead of everything else. I didn't care who got hurt. All I cared about was—

BRIE runs up to the podium.

BRIE: Not so fast. I have to set the record straight. I kidnapped Winston.

PEP SQUAD GIRL #1: Who?

OLIVE: She means Cappy.

BRIE: And I kidnapped him *twice.*

There is another gasp from the crowd and more exaggerated gasps from the PEP SQUAD.

BRIE (CONT'D): I'm really sorry.

PABLO: No, I did it, so I'm the one who's sorry.

OLIVE: Look, I did it, and I'm sorrier than both of you put together.

PRINCIPAL HIGGLEY: Whoa, whoa, whoa! What has gotten into you kids? As our mascot, Cappy is a symbol of all that Farley Middle School holds dear. Sportsmanship! Competition! Winning! I can't believe that any of you would want to destroy that—much less all of you.

OLIVE: But that's just it, Principal Higgley. Some of the kids who go to this school don't play sports.

PRINCIPAL HIGGLEY: Nonsense!

OLIVE: It's true. I know because . . . I'm one of them.

There is another gasp from the crowd and even more exaggerated gasps from the PEP SQUAD.

OLIVE (CONT'D): I know it might sound crazy, but the reason we took Cappy in the first place was to demand liberty and justice for all the kids who go to this school, not just the kids who swim laps and score points and cheer cheers and do whatever else the sporty kids do.

PEP SQUAD GIRL #2: You tell 'em, Henry!

OLIVE: (*Sighs*) Close enough.

PRINCIPAL HIGGLEY: I don't know what you're talking about. Farley Middle School is proud to support all our Capybaras in their extracurricular pursuits.

OLIVE: Really? Well, then why do all of us uncoordinated Capybaras have to hold our club meetings at the same time in the Dungeon?

PRINCIPAL HIGGLEY: Are you referring to the Academic Dimension? We created it as an innovative laboratory for creative collaboration.

PEP SQUAD GIRL #1:   More like a laboratory for the simultaneously study of auditory overstimulation, light deprivation, and site-specific crowd congestion.

PRINCIPAL HIGGLEY: I beg your pardon?

PEP SQUAD GIRL #2:   Principal Higgley, get with it. The Dungeon's dark, dank, and downright depressing. That's why Brendee and I joined the pep squad instead of the Math Maniacs. No one likes having to spend time down there.

PEP SQUAD GIRL #1:   Yeah, which is a real shame, because if me and Krystee were on the Math Maniacs, we'd be kicking some serious butt at the Math Decathlon this year.

OLIVE: Kids who don't play sports demand equal rights, equal attention, and equal practice space. Because separate—especially if it means sending us to the Dungeon—is never equal.

The student crowd cheers.

PEP SQUAD GIRL #1:   Hey, Henry, you really got this crowd on its feet. Ever think about coming out for pep squad?

OLIVE: It's actually Olive. Olive Henry. And, no. I mean, okay, I've *thought* about it. I even made up a little cheer, once. But I figured I'd get laughed off the field. There's sports kids and there's non-sports kids. It's pretty obvious which one I am.

PEP SQUAD GIRL #2:   Oh yeah? Did it ever occur to you that you might be, like, both?

OLIVE: Both?

PEP SQUAD GIRL #1:   Sure. I'm on pep squad, but like I said, my first love is math. I also do origami. I've got mad folding skills.

BOY #1:   Hey, me too. I like origami and football and Minecraft and stop-action animation.

BOY #2:   Dude, I like stop-action animation. And ice hockey, and anime.

BRIE: I like anime, too. I also like aikido and animal-rights activism. And I've always wanted to try Ultimate Frisbee.

OLIVE: Ultimate Frisbee?

BRIE nods sheepishly. A Frisbee is tossed her way, and she catches it.

OLIVE (CONT'D): Okay, awesome catch. And good point, too. The way I see it, everything we do makes Farley a better place, so we deserve the school's encouragement and support for *all* our efforts, not just those that hit the scoreboard.

There is a huge round of applause from the student body.

PRINCIPAL HIGGLEY: This has gone far enough. I have no idea where you got the idea that this school does not care about our students' artistic and other nonathletic pursuits.

YOGA KID: Well, you stick us in the Dungeon.

FRISBEE KID #2: (*On crutches*) And the auditorium— So many chairs!

BOY #2: Yeah, and on the announcements you never let us know when the musical tryouts are happening. I'm just sayin', some of us might have an inner "triple threat" to let out. (*He does a dance step and strikes a pose.*)

OLIVE: Be still my beating heart!

PRINCIPAL HIGGLEY: Now, see here. My job as a principal means I have to be both a prince and a pal to all students. I see nothing wrong with recognizing a wider range of student activities and exploring additional venues where they could potentially meet. Mrs. Delgado, can you organize a committee to study this and bring me some recommendations?

MRS. DELGADO: I'm on it, chief.

PRINCIPAL HIGGLEY: However, in the future, I would recommend that students bring such issues to my attention by visiting my office. Not by resorting to stunts like conspiring to kidnap our beloved mascot. Speaking of which, where is Cappy?

OLIVE: Yeah, so, about that. Cappy is in a better place now.

PEP SQUAD GIRL #1:   Oh no.

PEP SQUAD GIRL #2:   Poor Cappy!

OLIVE: No, wait. He's not dead. He's just much happier being a regular old capybara, not a school mascot.

PRINCIPAL HIGGLEY: But we have to have a school mascot. Or are you suggesting we go back to being the Fiddler Crabs?

SIXTH GRADER: Not the crab costume. Please, I'll do anything. Don't make me wear the crab costume!

OLIVE: Relax. I'm not suggesting we change our team name or our mascot.

PRINCIPAL HIGGLEY: You've lost me.

OLIVE: I know how important it is to everyone at Farley that we have a mascot that is as unique as our school. A mascot that stands out with quiet and majestic pride, like a capybara. But you know what makes a better mascot than an actual capybara? A capybara mascot who roller-skates! Say hello to our BRAND-NEW mascot!

REY, wearing a capybara costume and skates, rolls across the stage.

REYNALDO: 'Cause that's how I roll!

OLIVE: And who break-dances.

REYNALDO: Seriously? In the skates? Oh, all right.

REY demonstrates his prowess. The PEP SQUAD jumps up and down and applauds.

PEP SQUAD GIRL #1: (*Moved to tears*) I love that big furry guy.

PEP SQUAD GIRL #2: *(To Principal Higgley)* Can we keep him? Pleeeease?

PRINCIPAL HIGGLEY: Students, settle down. This has all been very . . . eye-opening. But I still don't understand. Where is Cappy? The original Cappy, that is.

BRIE: He is currently at a safe house. Tomorrow, he will be transported to an animal sanctuary in Virginia, where he will live out his days with a herd, in a setting that best meets his needs. His freedom was secured by the student organization P-CUDL—of which I am president—and supported by a generous grant from the Capybara Liberation Front.

PRINCIPAL HIGGLEY: Coach K., do you know anything about this?

COACH K.: *(Pulls out a wad of cash)* Put it this way: I can still visit my little buddy, and I now have the funds to expand my roster and include everyone who wants to play baseball. . . . Plus, Mrs. Delgado has offered to provide some extra study sessions for our team so no one has to choose between a great batting average and a great grade point average!

PRINCIPAL HIGGLEY: *(Throws his arms open to hug REY)* Welcome to Farley, new mascot!

The PEP SQUAD runs out and reprises their "you say Cappy" cheer. REY (dressed in his capybara costume) joins them, center stage.

BRIE: Olive, that was amazing! I'm sorry I ever doubted the power of your words to change the world.

OLIVE: *(Smiles)* I had a lot to work with. Your passion for animal rights is pretty inspiring.

BRIE: Omigosh, thanks for reminding me. I have to go update my website. My traffic has soared recently—nothing like a capybara crisis to drive student activists online! Catch up with you later?

OLIVE: Sure! I'll swing by the stables.

BRIE exits. OLIVE wanders over to MRS. DELGADO.

OLIVE (CONT'D): *(To MRS. DELGADO)* I really can't thank you enough for what you did at the zoo. If you hadn't picked up when I called, I don't know what would've happened.

MRS. DELGADO: I'll tell you what would've happened. I would have finished my Frappuccino! There's nothing like finally making your first solo trip to Starbucks in seven months and kicking back with *People* magazine . . . only to be interrupted by a frantic phone call from your son's best friend, who is ranting about an emergency involving stolen capybaras and escaped convicts.

OLIVE: Oh. When you put it like that . . . Sorry!

MRS. DELGADO: Please. Truth is, Olive, I'm like you. I live for drama. So? How'd I do in my role, Madame Playwright–slash–Director?

OLIVE: Very convincing. I can see where Rey gets his acting talent.

MRS. DELGADO: That's true. The dance moves he gets from his father.

They look over at REY, who is dancing up a storm with the PEP SQUAD.

OLIVE: (*With a sigh*) Well, now that I'm not going to Florida, I guess I'll have plenty of time to watch REY perform at Farley sporting events.

MRS. DELGADO: Not going to Florida? What are you talking about? I thought that playwriting competition was your dream—the big leagues! Don't tell me Principal Higgley made you withdraw from the competition.

OLIVE: No, he didn't. It was my choice. I cashed in my

plane ticket in order to make a generous contribution to the (*air quotes*) "Capybara Liberation Front."

MRS. DELGADO: You mean the money we gave to Coach K. to buy Cappy's freedom was . . .

OLIVE: Yup. Every last penny of it.

MRS. DELGADO: And the money you promised to give me to have my minivan cleaned after we take Cappy to the animal sanctuary this weekend?

OLIVE: Yeah, about that. Would you consider an IOU?

MRS. DELGADO: I've got a better idea. You can work off your debt helping out at the media center. Which, I might add, is an underutilized space after school. Might not be such a bad place to rehearse your plays.

OLIVE: Wow. That would be fantastic! I have a new play I'm working on, and that would be perfect. Thanks.

MRS. DELGADO: (*Shaking her head*) I still can't believe you cashed in your plane ticket. You worked so hard to get there, Olive. I mean, come on: the Super Bowl of scripting.

OLIVE: I know. It's funny. Last week, I would have given anything to go. But now, I don't need some contest to tell me that my voice matters. I have the chance to make a real difference right here. I guess it all boils down to something I've heard too many times to ignore: some things are more important.

MRS. DELGADO: Please tell me you're not talking about sports.

OLIVE: I'm not talking about sports.

MRS. DELGADO: Well, that's a relief. So, what's this new play of yours called?

OLIVE: I'm thinking about calling it *The Capybara Conspiracy.*

MRS. DELGADO: I like it. Be sure to save me a seat.

OLIVE: Will do, Mrs. D.

MRS. DELGADO winks at OLIVE, then exits. OLIVE skips back to the principal's office waiting-area chairs.

DEV: Wait a second. *The Capybara Conspiracy* is your new play?

OLIVE: That's the working title, yes.

DEV: So you're writing a play about everything that happened? With Cappy and Pablo and everything?

OLIVE: Something like that.

PRINCIPAL HIGGLEY enters immediately after.

PRINCIPAL HIGGLEY: Devin Bevins?

DEV: Yes? That's me.

PRINCIPAL HIGGLEY: Sorry to keep you waiting so long, son. I believe we have everything we need from your former school now. We'll just print you a copy of your schedule, and you can be on your way. Olive, thank you for waiting, too. I looked your script over, and I gotta say, it really kicks butt! That principal of yours is my favorite character. Love his line about being a prince and a pal!

OLIVE: Aw, thanks! I thought you might. Well, I should probably get to class. Nice to meet you, Dev. See you around.

OLIVE leaves quickly.

PRINCIPAL HIGGLEY: A lovely girl, that Olive. She's one of our brightest students. Did she tell you she was selected to represent our school in a national playwriting competition?

DEV: Yeah, she did. It's too bad she had to sell her plane ticket.

PRINCIPAL HIGGLEY: Sell her ticket? I don't follow.

DEV: You know, to buy Cappy's freedom.

PRINCIPAL HIGGLEY: Cappy?

DEV: Cappy the Capybara? The world's largest rodent and Farley Middle School's mascot, who happens to be an actual real live animal?

PRINCIPAL HIGGLEY: Cappy the Capybara?

DEV: Uh-huh.

PRINCIPAL HIGGLEY: Mrs. Delgado! Will you come out here, please?

MRS. DELGADO appears, carrying a stack of papers.

MRS. DELGADO: Yes, chief?

PRINCIPAL HIGGLEY: (*Looking concerned*) Have they been painting in the front hall today? I'm really wondering if the fumes might have gotten in here and affected . . .

DEV: (*To MRS. DELGADO*) Tell him! About you posing as an operative with the Capybara Liberation Front and intervening to rescue Winston.

MRS. DELGADO: Winston?

DEV: I mean Cappy! Cappy the Capybara! The world's largest rodent?

MRS. DELGADO and PRINCIPAL HIGGLEY exchange concerned looks.

MRS. DELGADO: *(Laughing nervously)* That's quite an imagination you have there, Devin. Perhaps you might like to join one of our many extracurricular clubs.

DEV: Oh, sure, in the Dungeon?

MRS. DELGADO: Dungeon? Oh, do you mean the lower level? Our clubs currently meet there because, as Principal Higgley just explained, we're doing some painting and renovations to our main level. *(She shifts gears and tries a new approach.)* So, Devin, I printed your new schedule. Would you like someone to show you to your homeroom?

She holds out a piece of paper to him. DEV grabs it from her.

DEV: No! I'm not going anywhere until someone explains what's really going on!

He balls up his new schedule and throws it across the room, just as COACH K. enters.

COACH K.: Say! That's quite an arm you've got on you there, kid! What's your name?

MRS. DELGADO: This is Devin Bevins, Coach. He just started here today.

DEV: (*Sullen*) Hello.

COACH K.: Nice to meet you, Devin. Come on by the batting cage after school if you're interested in checking out our baseball team. We could always use some new Crabs.

DEV: New what?

COACH K.: Crabs, kid. We're the Farley Fiddler Crabs. Funny name for a serious sports program! Here comes Crabby now, all suited up for today's game.

SIXTH GRADER, in crab costume, enters, walking sideways as before.

SIXTH GRADER: Scuttle, scuttle, scuttle. Hi, Coach K.!

MRS. DELGADO: (*To SIXTH GRADER*) Do me a favor— can you walk Devin here to his homeroom? (*She picks up the paper DEV threw, smooths it out, and hands it to him.*)

SIXTH GRADER: Sure! Walk this way.

DEV looks askance but follows, scuttling reluctantly.

PRINCIPAL HIGGLEY: (*Shaking his head*) Strange child. Oh, I almost forgot, Mrs. Delgado. Your son, Rey, and his friend Olive were here earlier.

MRS. DELGADO: Oh?

PRINCIPAL HIGGLEY: They wanted permission to try out some scenes from their new play at this week's pep rally.

MRS. DELGADO: What did you tell them?

PRINCIPAL HIGGLEY: I said yes, of course. After I botched the poor girl's name on the morning announcements last week, I figured I kind of owe her one. And I'm all for theater! As long as it doesn't get in the way of what's really important. You know, sports.

MRS. DELGADO: Oh yes, everyone at Farley knows how you feel about that. Did the kids tell you the name of their play?

PRINCIPAL HIGGLEY: Something dramatic about animals. *The Panda Pandemonium?* No, wait, is it *The Critter Crisis?*

MRS. DELGADO: *The Capybara Conspiracy?*

PRINCIPAL HIGGLEY: That's it! Wait, how did you know that?

MRS. DELGADO: *(Winking at OLIVE, who has snuck back in to grab an apple from the bowl)* Lucky guess.

OLIVE grins and takes a bite.

THE END

ABOUT
THE CAPYBARA CONSPIRACY

The Capybara Conspiracy is a novel. It is also, you may have noticed, a play. What this means is, in addition to reading it yourself, you can read it aloud with others or mount a dramatic production of it—it's really up to you. Here are some notes to help you.

Actors

It is often said that there are no small parts. That's not actually true, though the sentiment behind it is what theater is all about. Always make the most of whatever part you get. One person, no matter how great an actor he or she is, does not make a play. Unless it is a one-person show, which this is not.

In *The Capybara Conspiracy,* there are a *lot* of parts, some larger and some smaller. Many of the smaller parts can be played by the same actors, which means you have the flexibility to use a small cast (for example, thirteen people) or a larger one (twenty-four people or more). Also, many of the parts can be played by either a boy or a girl (e.g., Principal Higgley, Coach K., and many of the speaking parts in the ensemble). This gives you the flexibility to be inclusive in your casting choices.

Stage directions

These are provided in the book (before, after, and during the lines of dialogue). Sometimes they tell you specific things that will help make the story clearer to your audience. Sometimes, though, you may want or need to change things a little. Feel free to follow them or to disregard them (after first trying them) if you want to try to present things a different way. Part of theater is making choices, so if after trying it a few ways you decide there's a better choice for your stage or actors, go for it.

You'll notice that some of the stage directions are in parentheses. For example, those that appear with specific reference to an actor suggest how a line is said, like this:

OLIVE: (*Sarcastically*) Oh, really?

Other stage directions appear separately to tell you what's happening where, especially when the action shifts back and forth between two or more groups/settings, like this:

REY runs to the window, OLIVE trailing behind.

Three-act structure

As you've noticed by now, I'm sure, this play has three acts. When you stage it, if you have an intermission, you're going to want to have it after act II. It's also okay to not have an intermission, though you'll miss a good opportunity to serve snacks. Whatever you do, don't have two intermissions—this makes no sense to anyone and disrupts the flow of the play.

Stage crew

While you do not *need* a full stage crew to mount this as a play, it is handy to have a minimum of two kids who have *no* desire to be onstage yet would love to be involved in the production. This way, a lot of important jobs will get done well, like wrangling (that is actually the official term) costumes and props, and moving chairs and set pieces on- and offstage before and between scenes. What is helpful to everyone is to use masking tape ahead of time to mark the floor where the chairs and set pieces go. The audience won't notice, and you'll get these things on and off swiftly and consistently, which helps avoid unnecessary interruptions in the story and action. Also, if the backstage kids want a little time onstage, they can be part of the pep-rally scene toward the end, which can always benefit from a few extra kids.

Lighting and sound

If you're doing a full dramatic production and you have the capability to use microphones and stage lights to full advantage, by all means go for it. However, you don't need these things to do a staged reading. Remember that the whole point of amplification is to ensure that your audience can hear the actors—otherwise the story will really be lost on them (and audiences who can't hear actors often end up getting loud, which compounds the problem). So if you need it, set it up and practice with it. If you don't need it, don't complicate matters, but do work with your actors on speaking clearly and loudly and on looking at the audience rather than their shoes. Same goes for lighting. There are several references to spotlights and bare bulbs, which are used to focus attention on the characters and set the stage for the events portrayed. You can achieve a similar effect by dimming the regular lights and positioning a stage-crew member with a flashlight to shine strategically (from above, so as not to blind the actor). Another option is to have the actor onstage but frozen until the key moment, then start talking and moving when it's his or her turn before freezing again, which creates the effect of coming to life, much as a spotlight does.

Props, costumes, and sets

To stage *The Capybara Conspiracy*, you can certainly go all out and create complicated props, costumes, and sets. Feel free to reenvision the whole thing taking place on a boat in a hurricane and rent a wind machine to get the right effect—you have my blessing. However, if you want to keep it simple, that is often for the best. There's so much you can do with minimal staging. For example, on page 92, panto-mime pressing the doorbell buzzer and make the noise, and the other actor will pantomime opening the door. And on page 130, a set of chairs makes a great minivan. Buckle up! You really only need a few things to pull this off:

- **Some chairs,** like the ones you'd find in a classroom (you'll need two chairs for the principal's office waiting area, plus about eight additional chairs to configure as classroom settings, the interrogation chairs, Mrs. Delgado's minivan, etc.).
- **An archway.** A what? I am calling this an archway because that is the only word that comes to mind for what I am about to describe. Basically what I mean is some way of sectioning off an area to convey to your audience that it is a small, enclosed space. You can create this by attaching two long sticks or rods to two chairs, placing them a distance apart, stringing some sort of rope to connect them, and hanging a sign from it. This can be used for several parts of the play that take place in specific spots, like the broom closet, Brie's stables/garage, and the Delgado family's bathroom.
- **And speaking of signs . . .** Through the creative use of paper and pens, you can assist your audience tremendously. As noted on page 1, you need a sign on the wall behind the principal's office waiting area that says

PRINCIPAL'S OFFICE—WAIT HERE. If you want to get funny/creative, add one of those PLEASE TAKE A NUMBER signs below it or a goofy motivational poster like that one with the cat clinging to a tree branch. There are also signs that have roles in the play, like the sign outside the middle school that has an actual walk-on role (and the zoo signs, similarly, can be carried on), so be sure to use signs to their fullest advantage to ensure your audience stays connected with the story you're telling.

- **Costumes.** Most of the characters in this play are middle school kids, so no special costumes are needed. However, costume pieces can be a lot of fun to use strategically to bring characters and events to life. For example, the pep squad can carry pom-poms with them at all times—this serves the dual purpose of showing how dedicated they are to school spirit *and* having the pom-poms available to them, since they occasionally break into cheers. The crab costume worn by an embarrassed sixth grader is a visual joke, so it does not need to be elaborate, but it does need to exist so your audience gets the joke.

- **Props.** Most of the props in this play are items that should be easy to find, like an apple and a baseball. Ideally, one person should be in charge of props, to make sure you get or make everything you need and to keep track of these items when they are not onstage.

- **Cappy.** As you'll notice, *The Capybara Conspiracy* features Cappy the Capybara, who is an actual, real live capybara (otherwise known as the world's largest rodent). I cannot stress this enough: YOU DO NOT NEED

TO OBTAIN AN ACTUAL, REAL LIVE CAPYBARA TO STAGE THIS PLAY. Nor should you, unless you happen to have a pet capybara that is docile and aspires to be on the stage. I take that back: even if you *do* have a pet capybara that fits this description, *don't* cast him in this play. Your options are: (1) cast a kid in the role of Cappy, or (2) use an object—like a cardboard or wooden two-dimensional capybara or a papier-mâché three-dimensional capybara you built or assembled for this project after researching capybaras to ensure it actually resembles one!—for the role (and have his "lines" voiced by a kid offstage). I'm guessing some of you will be tempted to give his part to another animal, like a very generously proportioned guinea pig or another obscure, largish rodent, like a muskrat or nutria (look it up) or a dog who bears an unfortunate resemblance to a capybara. This is a *bad* idea. Animals should not be asked to do these kinds of things (you do realize this was one of the points made by the book, yes?). Plus, no matter what your dog/guinea pig/muskrat/nutria looks like, I guarantee it cannot actually pass for a capybara. I'm all for inclusive casting when it comes to kids, but when it comes to animals, not so much.

Character list

- Olive Henry (seventh-grade girl)
- Devin Bevins (the new kid)

- Reynaldo "Rey" Delgado (seventh-grade boy)
- Pablo Fuentes (seventh-grade boy)
- Gabriella "Brie" Greenberg (eighth-grade girl)
- Pep Squad Girl #1 (aka Brendee)
- Pep Squad Girl #2 (aka Krystee)
- Boy #1 (aka Bradley Dupree)
- Boy #2 ("triple threat")
- Sixth Grader (aka Crabby the Fiddler Crab)
- Coach K.
- Mrs. Delgado (Rey's mother)
- Principal Higgley
- Flags #1–3 (can be played by actors playing multiple parts)
- Che Guevara (can be played by an actor playing multiple parts)
- 4–8 Dungeon Kids (Yoga Kid[s], Math Maniac[s], and Orff Ensemble Kids—can be played by actors playing multiple parts)
- 2 Frisbee Kids (can be played by actors playing multiple parts)
- Maya Delgado (Rey's sister)
- Luis Fuentes (Pablo's brother)
- Mrs. Fuentes (Pablo's mother)
- Sign/Newscaster/Jail Recording/Capybara Liberation Front (can be played by actors playing multiple parts)
- Cappy (can be a prop, with lines voiced by an actor off-stage)

Bibliography

If you're interested in theater and/or capybaras, here are some books you might enjoy.

- *Acting for Young Actors: The Ultimate Teen Guide,* by Mary Lou Belli and Dinah Lenney. A book of acting exercises and examples of ways to think about theater, research characters, improvise, think like an actor, and more
- *Acting Out.* Six one-act plays by six Newbery-winning authors
- *Better Nate Than Ever* and *Five, Six, Seven, Nate!,* both by Tim Federle. Novels about a boy who is an aspiring Broadway actor and his adventures seeking fame, fortune, and fun, onstage and off
- *The BFG: A Set of Plays.* One of five novels by Roald Dahl that have been adapted into plays "with useful tips on staging, props, and costumes." The others include *Charlie and the Chocolate Factory* and *James and the Giant Peach.*
- *Capyboppy.* Has *The Capybara Conspiracy* made you curious about what it would be like to have a Cappy of your own? Author and illustrator Bill Peet actually kept a capybara as a pet and wrote this book about the experience.
- *Drama,* by Raina Telgemeier. A graphic novel about a middle school kid who loves theater but prefers stage crew to being in the spotlight
- *Good Masters! Sweet Ladies!* A set of monologues voiced by characters from a medieval village, by Laura Amy Schlitz

ACKNOWLEDGMENTS

Thank *you* for reading this book. I want to give a special shout-out to those of you who read some or all of it out loud—or helped out backstage so that others could do so—whether as part of an actual dramatic performance or not. I also want to give a standing ovation to the librarians and teachers and authors and bloggers and booksellers (not to mention my family members and friends) and, most importantly, kids who have given my books a home on their shelves and then, even better, have gushed about them to other readers. There's nothing better than a heartfelt book endorsement from someone you trust. If you love this book—or any book—thanks so much for telling people about it.

Thanks to the hugely talented Walter Mayes and Karen Harris (who, while shorter than Walter, is no less talented), both of whom provided invaluable assistance with the theatrical aspects of this book. Thanks also to Roxana Barillas,

Meg Medina, and Charles Girard for being on my team of astute advisers. Thanks to the Virginia Center for the Creative Arts (VCCA) and the DC Commission on the Arts and Humanities for supporting my work. Thanks to my dear friends at First Book (make some noise, PAR!) for their camaraderie, love, and support, as well as for the important work they do every day to get books to kids in need. Seriously, check them out: www.firstbook.org.

Thanks to my awesome agent, Carrie Hannigan, and everyone at HSG for championing a novel that didn't look like a regular novel, and to everyone at Knopf and Penguin Random House, especially my amazing editor, Erin Clarke, who encouraged me to tell this story in the way that made the most sense to me (which, thankfully, also made sense to her). Thanks to my wonderful community of DC writers and readers, which includes the Children's Book Guild and the DC Women Writers Group and my beloved book club. . . . I feel so lucky to have several overlapping circles of fabulous, talented, caring, and interesting people to eat, drink, laugh, and schmooze with (and commiserate with when I'm stuck). I am also grateful for Sczerina Perot, Rebecca Kasemeyer, and Jenny Smulson, aka my Extreme Runner buddies. Thanks for keeping me company, keeping me sane, putting up with my crazy dogs, and helping me burn off all the candy I eat. And speaking of dogs, thanks to Clover and Penny, the two most wonderful distractions a writer could ever hope for. I would not trade either of you for a capybara, and that's saying something.

Most of all, thanks to Mike, Franny, and Bougie. I love you guys to the moon and back. Also, FWAKAH!!!

Application for permission to perform the play may be made through the author's agent, Carrie Hannigan, at:
Hannigan Salky Getzler Agency
37 W. 28th Street, 8th Floor
New York, NY 10001;
or via email to channigan@hsgagency.com.

ABOUT THE AUTHOR

Erica S. Perl is the author of *When Life Gives You O.J., Aces Wild, Vintage Veronica,* and a number of picture books. She lives in Washington, D.C., where she works at First Book, the groundbreaking organization that provides books to children in need. SHE'S SUPER COOL. Sorry, that's me, Olive, again—just had to get that in. Learn more about Erica at EricaPerl.com.